The Superhero's Team

Second book in The Superhero's Son

By Lucas Flint

An Annulus Publishing Book

Annulus Publishing, Cherokee, Texas, 2016

Published by Secret Identity Books. An imprint of Annulus Publishing.

Contact: luke@lucasflint.com

Cover design by Damonza (https://damonza.com/)

ISBN-13: 978-1534978188

ISBN-10: 1534978186

CHAPTER ONE

HOW CAN SOMEONE SO big, so heavy, and so obnoxious be so hard to find?

I creeped along the roof of a building, doing my best not to be noticed by the huge crowd of screaming and shouting people below. There were hundreds of people, maybe even thousands, and they were all packed in the same street venue, waving American flags and wearing blue hats with the words 'MAKE AMERICA NORMAL AGAIN' in white lettering. Men in dark suits wearing sunglasses and carrying holstered guns at their sides stood at various points around the area of the rally, mostly around the entrances or exits, and I knew there were probably also Secret Service agents in the other buildings, too. On the stage in front of everyone was a tall podium, with two large American flags standing behind it. Dozens of reporters from all the major news networks and websites had preferential space in front of the stage to cover the event, but it was impossible to tell what they were saying due to the loud cheering and screaming of the crowd.

Frankly, I was surprised at how many people had gathered

here in Fallsville, Texas today. It was a city of maybe 15,000 and it never drew crowds this large for anyone, but I guess that Adam Lucius Plutarch—the head of Plutarch Industries, current presidential nominee, and formerly known as the supervillain the Billionaire—really was as popular as everyone said he was. I didn't see him on stage yet, but he was most likely going to appear soon.

I wasn't here for Plutarch, however. I was here because I was searching for a minor supervillain who, like any self-respecting minor supervillain who usually worked as a lackey for more major villains like Manifest, had robbed a bank in Fallsville. His name was Steel Skin, so named because his skin was like steel. He was also big enough to pick me up and throw me around like a rag doll. Ask me how I know.

The only reason I was after him was because I happened to be in town to buy my first car from a dealership, because I was going to college next year and would need a car of my own to get there. But I sort of forgot about that when I saw Steel Skin running down the street with a huge bag of money over his shoulder and the police ineffectually shooting him with their guns in an attempt to stop him.

So, like any burgeoning superhero, I suited up and went after him. I actually managed to corner him, but then he threw me around like a rag doll (see above) and somehow managed to disappear after that. I saw him running in the direction of this Plutarch rally, so I came here to find him, thinking he might try to either blend in with the crowd or maybe cause a scene and escape in the chaos.

That brought us back to my current predicament: Where the

hell did he go?

Seriously, there was no way that a man as huge and burly as Steel Skin could hide near a rally as huge and loud as a Plutarch rally. There were Secret Service agents everywhere, for one, and likely some G-Men, too, but I didn't see any. Not that that surprised me, considering Plutarch's well-known anti-neohero rhetoric and his promise to 'make America normal again.' I wasn't sure how he intended to do that, but it wasn't my job to make sense of his political platform. I just needed to stop Steel Skin before he hurt anyone.

I tapped the earcom in my ear and whispered, “Val, have your sensors found Steel Skin yet?”

“Negative,” said Valerie, who was technically the personal AI assistant of my Dad, but she also helped me because I was his son, “although the huge amount of people present makes it difficult, almost impossible, to locate him or any other individual.”

I sighed. “Looks like I'm going to have to look for him the old-fashioned way, then. But do you know if Steel Skin happens to have any other powers besides his tough skin and super strength? Like teleportation or invisibility, perhaps?”

“Again, negative, Bolt,” said Valerie. “His Neo Ranks page states that he has only two known powers. And at the age of thirty, he is well-beyond neohero puberty, so he is unlikely to spontaneously develop any other powers out of the blue.”

“Then maybe he is using some kind of technology to hide himself,” I said, cringing at a particularly sudden shout from the crowd below. “Stole something from the government, maybe?”

“Unknown,” said Valerie. “It is possible that he has an

accomplice. He has been known to serve the supervillain Manifest and the Earth King in the past and has allied with other villains such as the Programmer."

I groaned. "So I might have to fight *two* villains, then. That will be fun."

"It is only a theory," said Valerie. "Nonetheless, I suggest you keep your eyes open. Even villains as dim-witted as Steel Skin can occasionally have moments of cleverness."

I nodded. "All right. I'll just—"

I was interrupted by sudden shouting in the streets. I looked over the edge of the building and saw another huge crowd of people—this one lacking any American flags or MANA hats—approaching the rally. This crowd was almost as huge as the one in the rally, but they carried signs with them that said things like 'PLUTARCH IS A BIGOT' and 'PLUTARCH FOR PRISON 2016.' The protestors in that crowd sounded really angry, shouting and screaming and waving their signs so crazily that I was worried that the signs might go flying out of their hands and hit someone if they weren't careful. At the head of the protesting crowd was a fat girl who looked to be about my age, but had weird green hair and had very short hair that was almost completely shaven off, which made me feel sick when I saw it.

"What is that?" I said, staring at the protestors, who looked like an army on the move, albeit a very messy and disorganized one.

"Anti-Plutarch protestors," said Valerie. "According to the news, Plutarch's rallies have been plagued by large crowds of protestors who disagree with his policies and do not believe he would make a good President."

"So they're just here to protest Plutarch, then," I said.

"Presumably," said Valerie. "Unfortunately, many of Plutarch's rallies have been marred by conflicts between his supporters and his protestors. They have never led to any deaths, but many people usually get hurt."

"Just great," I said, looking from the loud crowd of anti-Plutarch protestors and the Plutarch supporters gathered before the stage. "If a riot starts, Steel Skin will probably use it to escape. I can't let him do that."

"Didn't your father say that you aren't supposed to be hunting down supervillains?" said Valerie. "Genius has repeatedly said that you should focus on your studies, not on fighting crime or bringing supervillains to justice."

"I know, I know, but there aren't any other neoheroes in Silvers or Fallsville and Steel Skin is a threat to normal people who the police can't stop, so I've got to stop him no matter what," I said.

"Then I will have to report you to your father," said Valerie. "Genius will not be happy to learn about this."

"Do what you want," I said, looking around the area for any sign of Steel Skin. "When I get home, I'll tell Dad—"

Once more, I was interrupted, but this time from the Plutarch supporters, who had suddenly burst into even louder cheers and screams. I thought at first that Steel Skin had attacked the crowd, but then I noticed a man was walking on stage.

The man was tall, probably six foot two, and he wore a very expensive-looking black suit. He was probably in his late sixties, but he didn't look it, because he stood and walked upright like a much younger man. He appeared to be wearing a blonde wig of some kind, though no one in the crowd seemed to care, because they were screaming at him like he was a rock star. He waved at the crowd, his large smile and white teeth visible even from a distance.

"Is that Adam Plutarch?" I said, watching as the man walked over to the front of the podium, which had bullet-proof glass barriers in front of it.

"Affirmative," said Valerie. "Founder and CEO of Plutarch Industries, among hundreds of other Plutarch brand businesses. He is one of the two major presidential nominees for the office of President of the United States, running against the opposing nominee Barnabas Sagan. He was also the supervillain the Billionaire, though he retired from supervillainy eleven years ago."

This was the first time I'd seen Plutarch in person. He didn't look that different from other big businessmen I'd seen, so I didn't understand why the people were going crazy over him. "How do we know he really isn't a supervillain anymore?"

"According to his Neo Ranks page, he has worked with the G-Men to put several of his old supervillain colleagues behind bars, such as the Vile Four," said Valerie. "But not everyone in the neohero community believes he has truly reformed. Some think it's just an act, but no one knows for sure."

I nodded. "Well, it looks like he's about to make a speech. And since I hate political speeches and don't see Steel Skin anywhere, I think we should leave. Maybe Steel Skin didn't come here."

"Agreed," said Valerie. "You should probably go back to the dealership and get your car, just like your father told you to do."

I rolled my eyes. “Valerie, you're even worse than Mom sometimes, you know that?”

“Your father simply expects me to make sure you don't put yourself in unnecessary danger,” said Valerie. “He just wants you to live a normal life.”

I was about to say that I couldn't live a 'normal' life if I could knock down buildings with a single punch when I noticed a couple of Secret Service agents speaking to each other. They looked to the left side of the stage, like they saw something, but before they could draw their guns, a massive, shirtless man—with skin that shone like polished steel—burst onto stage screaming. He knocked aside the two Secret Service agents like bowling pins and ran at Plutarch screaming.

“There he is,” said Valerie in my ear dryly.

I shot off the roof of the building, flying through the air at super speed, people gasping and pointing at me from below. I landed hard on the stage, creating a small crater, in between Steel Skin and Plutarch.

“Hey!” Steel Skin shouted, skidding to a stop in front of me. He towered above me, his thick steel skin reflecting the light of the sun above. He pointed at me. “Get out of the way, pipsqueak. Plutarch is mine.”

“Sorry, but I already let you get away with stealing from a bank,” I said. “If I let you get away with murder, I'd have to hang up my suit and buy a car.”

“Do I look like I care?” said Steel Skin, his voice rumbling. “Move or I'll use you as a stick to beat Plutarch with.”

“No way,” I said, shaking my head. I glanced over my shoulder at Plutarch, who still stood there behind me. “Mr.

Plutarch, are you all right?"

Plutarch shook his head and looked confident again. "Of course I am, kid. He didn't even touch me."

"You won't be in a second, Plutarch," Steel Skin growled. He pointed over my head at Plutarch. "I'm going to get you for betraying us, you bastard!"

"Betraying?" I said.

"Ah," said Valerie in my ear. "According to Steel Skin's Neo Ranks page, he once belonged to a supervillain team called the Vile Four, organized and funded by Adam Plutarch. Apparently, every member of the Vile Four is currently in jail, thanks to Plutarch's working with the G-Men to capture them."

"Except Steel Skin, obviously," I muttered. "Looks like we got a good old revenge motive, then."

Then I said to Steel Skin, "I don't care why you want him dead. If you want to get to him, you'll have to go through me first."

Steel Skin's hands balled into fists. "All right, kid, I'll beat you into paste and then turn Plutarch into paste, too, and mix you together so no one knows who is who!"

I was about to say that that was gross and didn't really make any sense, but then Steel Skin's fists came flying at me like cannonballs. I caught them and held Steel Skin back with my super strength while a couple of Secret Service agents escorted Plutarch off the stage. People in the crowds below screamed and cameras flashed, but I didn't pay attention to them. I just had to get Steel Skin away from here, because I knew that any fight between me and him would put the lives of innocent people at risk.

Steel Skin was strong, but I held my ground. We struggled against each other before Steel Skin suddenly headbutted me. It was like being hit by a crowbar, briefly dazing me long enough for Steel Skin to pick me up and slam me through the stage floor.

I crashed onto the street underneath the stage, stunned by the blow. I saw Steel Skin jump over the hole, which meant he was going after Plutarch. Shaking my head, I flew up through the hole and tackled Steel Skin in the back, knocking him to the stage floor before he could get far.

"Get off me, you stupid kid," said Steel Skin, grabbing at me on his back, but I was small enough that he couldn't reach me.

"Nope," I said, shaking my head. "Not until you promise to go to jail quietly."

Steel Skin growled and then rolled over onto his back, which meant that I now found myself being crushed underneath his massive bulk. I gasped for air, letting go of him, causing Steel Skin to stand up and run away.

I thought he was going after Plutarch again, so I rose to my feet, but then I saw him rip the podium off the stage and hurl it at me. I had only enough time to say, "Uh oh," before the podium slammed into me with the force of a car. I was sent flying through the back of the stage, knocking down several American flags in the process, which caught and tangled me in their cloth.

Oh, god, my head was so dizzy, but then I heard bullets being fired and immediately snapped back to normal. I stood up, tore the American flags off my body, and flew into the air above the rally.

Below, I saw Plutarch enter a large black car, while Steel Skin was running toward it. A couple of Secret Service agents—who were either really brave or really dumb—were shooting bullets at him, but the bullets just deflected off of Steel Skin's body harmlessly. He knocked them both aside like flies just as the engine for the car revved.

But before Plutarch's car could go, Steel Skin grabbed its back and held it tight. The car's wheels screeched against the pavement, but the car didn't even budge under Steel Skin's grip. He grunted and tipped the car over onto its side, causing its wheels to spin uselessly in the air. Then Steel Skin climbed on top of the overturned car, probably intending to pull Plutarch out of it.

I wasn't going to let him, so I shot through the air and body-slammed Steel Skin, sending him flying off the side of the car. He hit the pavement and rolled for several feet until he crashed into another car that had no people in it, where he lay with a stunned look on his face.

Landing on the street between Plutarch's car and Steel Skin, I said, "Look, man, we could do this all day, but I've got things to do and you've got things to do, so why don't we just call it a day?"

Steel Skin grunted. He stood up slowly, but then grabbed the car he had smashed into and brought it down on me. I had no time to dodge, so I raised my hands to protect myself from the impact.

At the last second, however, the car exploded into a flock of white birds. The birds flew away into the sky, chirping happily and peacefully, while Steel Skin and I looked after them in disbelief.

"Huh?" said Steel Skin, staring at the birds, dumbfounded. "What happened to that car?"

I was wondering the same thing. That, and if there was any car insurance company in the country that covered 'car turning into a flock of white birds.' Maybe it went under 'Acts of God.'

Steel Skin shook his head and glared at me. "Did you do that? One of your stupid powers or something?"

I held up my hands. "Hey, I'm just as surprised by this as you are. Maybe that's a sign from God that you're not supposed to try to assassinate presidential candidates who put your criminal friends behind bars."

Steel Skin grunted again. He ran at me, but then a rope flew out of nowhere and wrapped around his legs. Steel Skin slammed into the street face-first, which would have made me feel bad for him if he hadn't been trying to kill me.

"What the hell?" said Steel Skin, looking at the rope tied securely around his ankles. "Where did this come from?"

"That would be me," said a voice somewhere above me.

I looked up just in time to see a girl floating down through the air toward me. She looked to be about my age, with long, blonde hair, a purple domino mask, and a cape and robes to match it. She had a magician's wand in her hand, a wand that was currently glowing with energy. She was actually kind of hot, even though her robes and cape didn't let me see much.

As the mysterious girl landed, Steel Skin snapped the ropes binding his legs and stood up. He pointed at the girl, who stood a few feet away from me and seemed unconcerned that a giant shirtless man was pointing threateningly at her.

"You!" said Steel Skin. "Did you turn that car into pigeons?"

The girl sighed. "They're *doves*, not *pigeons*. Not that I expect a man of your mental capacity to be able to tell the difference, but I feel it's important to keep this distinction clear."

Hot *and* sarcastic? Sign me up.

"Who cares about a bunch of birds?" said Steel Skin. He punched his fist into his hand. "I'll turn both of you into paste just the same."

Steel Skin ran at us. I made a move to meet him, but the girl waved her wand and said, "I got this. You just sit back and watch."

Before I could ask her how she was going to stop 300 pounds of pure steel and stupidity, the girl waved her wand again and pointed it at Steel Skin.

Immediately, a huge titanium box appeared out of nowhere and clamped tightly around Steel Skin, leaving only his head exposed. Steel Skin tried to break free, but even I could tell that his strength, as great as it was, was no match for the box that held him.

"There," said the girl, lowering her wand and smiling satisfactorily. "Easy."

"I was expecting something a bit … more fantastic than a box," I said, putting my hands on my hips and looking at Steel Skin (who was now shouting all kinds of curses at us) with disappointment. "Like an explosion or something."

"Sometimes the simplest solution is best," said the girl. "Steel Skin won't be getting out of there until I want him to. And by the time I want him to, he should be safely behind bars in Ultimate Max prison where he belongs."

I nodded. "Right. Well, uh, what's your name? I'm—"

"Bolt," the girl finished for me. She smiled. "I've heard of you."

"You have?" I said. "But we've never met."

"Your fight with Master Chaos last month was streamed all

over the world," said the girl. "Everyone saw it."

"Ah," I said. "That's right. I almost forgot. Well, now that you know my name, it's time for you to tell me your name."

"Incantation," said the girl simply. "I am the apprentice of Thaumaturge. You've heard of him, right?"

"Yeah," I said. "He's one of the leaders of the Neohero Alliance, right?"

"Yep," said Incantation, "and he taught me everything I know about magic, though he's not here at the moment."

"You can use magic?" I said. "Real magic? I thought our powers were genetic."

Incantation looked like she was about to say something before a loud, boisterous voice behind us shouted, "Hey, kid! Good job!"

Incantation and I looked over to see Adam Plutarch—whose slightly crooked wig was the only indication that his car had been turned over—walking toward me with a couple of Secret Service agents in tow. He didn't seem even slightly fazed by the fact that a giant shirtless man with metal skin had just tried to kill him; then again, as a former supervillain, he'd probably seen far stranger things.

As Plutarch approached, I noticed Incantation step away. She was glaring at Plutarch like he had insulted her mother, even though Plutarch wasn't even looking at her.

"Amazing, simply amazing," said Plutarch. He looked over our heads at Steel Skin, who was still cursing up a storm. "I have never seen such an efficient defeat of a loser like him." He looked down at me with a big smile. "Good job, kid. If I knew your real identity, I'd offer you a paid internship at the White House after I win the election."

"Oh, that's, er, generous of you, Mr. Plutarch, but it was really Incantation here who beat him," I said, gesturing at Incantation. "I could barely hold him back."

Plutarch's big, friendly smile vanished as soon as he looked at Incantation. Incantation met his gaze, even though Plutarch was much bigger and stronger than her.

"Incantation, huh?" said Plutarch. He didn't sound nearly as friendly as he had a moment before. "Apprentice of Thaumaturge, right?"

"Yes," said Incantation, which was the only word she said.

"Well, then," said Plutarch, his tone colder. "Thanks for the help. I make a point of thanking the people who save my life, however I may feel about other people they know, so thank you."

Incantation didn't say anything. She just folded her arms across her chest and glared at Plutarch, who held her gaze for a moment before looking at me again. There was clearly some bad history between them, or at least between Plutarch and her master, though I didn't know much about it.

"Anyway, my men here have already called the police and contacted the G-Men to take Steel Skin away, so you two can leave now," said Plutarch, waving in a random direction like he didn't care where we went.

"Um, all right," I said. "Then I guess we'll—"

"Hold on," said Plutarch, interrupting me suddenly. He leaned closer to me. "Hey, you're Bolt, right? That kid who defeated Master Chaos?"

"Yes, sir," I said. "That's me. Why?"

Plutarch's smile widened considerably, which made him look kind of creepy. "Most kids your age don't have that kind of accomplishment under their belt. I think you're going places, kid. And if you ever need any wisdom gained from a lifetime of success, just give me a call."

Plutarch drew a card out of his front pocket and handed it to me before I even realized what was going on. I looked down at the card and saw that it had Plutarch's name and contact information written on it.

"All right," said Plutarch. He gave me the thumbs up. "See you later, kid. Never stop dreaming!"

With that, Plutarch turned and walked away, with the two Secret Service agents following behind him. I didn't know what to say to that. I just looked at Incantation, who had folded her arms over her chest and looked incredibly displeased.

"Um …" I said. "Want to go out sometime?"

Incantation looked at me like I had just said something stupid. Then she shook her head and said, "No, but I would like to talk with you about something, about the reason I helped you beat Steel Skin."

"Talk?" I said. "About what?"

"Let's go find some place private to talk and I'll tell you there," said Incantation. "I don't want Plutarch or his goons listening in on our conversation."

I looked over at Plutarch, who was now talking with people who appeared to be his campaign advisers, and then looked at Incantation again. "Sure. I've got time. Let's go."

CHAPTER TWO

MOM ALWAYS TOLD ME that I should be very careful about the girls who I hang out with. She always stressed that I shouldn't be alone with a girl I barely knew for any reason. Dad also always said more or less the same thing. Yeah, they didn't talk about it so much since I became seventeen, but every now and then they'd remind me not to be too girl crazy.

But come on, how many other guys get a chance to talk with the (very hot) apprentice of one of the most famous neoheroes in the country? And anyway, we technically weren't *really* alone. We chose to talk on top of a building far away from the Plutarch rally, which gave us some privacy, but it wasn't really *that* private. I mean, I could have punched a hole through the roof and probably ended up in some guy's apartment, which, in my opinion, satisfied the criteria my parents set for 'never spend time alone with a strange girl you don't know.'

So we stood on the apartment building's roof, with Incantation leaning against the entrance to the roof and I standing opposite her. The wind was blowing really hard today, and it was cold, too, but Incantation hardly seemed bothered by it, even though the wind was causing her hair to flap around crazily until she pulled her hood over her head.

"All right," I said. "We're alone. What do you want to talk about?"

"I want to make you an offer," said Incantation. "Have you heard of the Young Neos before?"

"Oh, yeah," I said. "They're the team made up of young up-and-coming neoheroes, right?"

"Correct," said Incantation. "There are five of us at the moment, but we're always looking for new members. But we have very high standards for our members, so we can't just let anyone join."

"I read about you guys on Neo Ranks," I said. "You're the leader."

"That is also correct," said Incantation, though she was starting to sound impatient, like I was missing something. "Normally, we send an invitation to prospective members, but I decided to come to Texas myself to personally invite you to join the Young Neos."

I put my hands on my chest. "Wait, you want *me* to join the Young Neos? Why me? I'm not any special. I'm just an ordinary teen … well, okay, I can punch down buildings and fly through the sky like a bullet, but I'm still nothing special."

"The reason I am inviting you is because of your defeat of Master Chaos last month," said Incantation.

"But I didn't do that on my own," I said. "My dad, Genius, helped a lot."

"True, but it takes a lot of courage for a new hero like yourself to go toe-to-toe with a highly experienced and dangerous villain like Master Chaos and survive," said Incantation. "That's exactly the sort of courage we're looking for in new recruits. We saw your livestream of the fight and got a good look at your skills and resourcefulness."

I was glad I was wearing my suit, which mostly covered my face, because I was starting to blush at Incantation's praise. She probably said that sort of thing to every new member they approached, but I still enjoyed it.

"So you came down to Texas specifically to look for me?" I said.

"Pretty much," said Incantation. She wrinkled her nose. "Otherwise I wouldn't come to this stupid part of the country."

Her sudden harshness caught me by surprise. "What?"

"Never mind," said Incantation. "And don't worry about whether I got permission from the NHA. I spoke with my master, Thaumaturge, about it, and he approved my trip to Texas to offer you membership in the Young Neos."

"Cool," I said. "But what, exactly, does membership in the Young Neos entail? If I joined, would I get a new costume or something?"

"No," said Incantation. "We'd get a patch to put on your costume with the Young Neos emblem, but you would otherwise just wear your normal suit."

"Awesome," I said. "What other perks do I get?"

"You'll have a chance to join the NHA itself if you do well enough," said Incantation. "You'll also have access to all of the NHA's training facilities, so you will be able to go to Hero Island any time you want and train there."

"Cool," I said. "Do you have a headquarters or something?"

"We do have a base on Hero Island," said Incantation, "so yes, we do have a headquarters. It's called the House."

"And cool team vehicles that can fly you all over the world to fight evil wherever it needs to be fought?" I said.

"Yes," said Incantation, nodding. "All paid for by the NHA, but I have to warn you that it isn't all easy. We're always on the move, fighting crime wherever we need to go, and clashing with supervillains all the time."

"Like Steel Skin," I said. "Right?"

"Right," said Incantation. "But we don't have the complete freedom to do what we like. Although I'm the leader, we're still under the supervision of the NHA. We can only go on missions approved by my master and can't pick and choose which ones we use."

"Why do you need supervision?" I asked.

"Because we're still teenagers," said Incantation. "The NHA doesn't think we're mature enough to lead ourselves just yet. So we need the supervision of our master to make sure we don't get into trouble."

I hesitated when she said that. I liked my independence. Granted, I didn't have *real* independence, since I still lived with my parents and all, but it wasn't like I had to report to a superior or whatever. Still, the idea of having access to the Hero Island training facilities, plus all of their amenities, and going around the world fighting crime with other heroes myself was very tempting, to put it mildly.

"But what about school?" I said. "Don't any of you guys have to go to class and get your homework and stuff?"

"We have tutors," said Incantation. "Since we're all neoheroes in training, we can't really go to normal schools without affecting our grades or risking our secret identities. So we have tutors who work with our erratic schedules."

"Erratic?" I said. "What do you mean?"

"Crime doesn't exactly follow a set schedule," said Incantation. "Sometimes a supervillain is terrorizing a city and we have to leave as soon as possible to stop him. Or maybe another supervillain is going to nuke the moon in the middle of the night, so we have to get up and go after him even if we're asleep."

"Someone tried to nuke the moon?" I said. "When did that happen?"

Incantation shook her head. "IThe point is that we'd never be in school if we went, so we have tutors who are available pretty much whenever we need them."

"Would I get a tutor if I joined?" I said.

"Of course," said Incantation. "Every member of the Young Neos has one."

That took care of that problem, but I was still hesitant about joining. I thought about what Mom and Dad might say if I came home and told them that I had joined a superhero team.

"What about my parents?" I said. "Do I need their permission to join?"

"No," said Incantation, "but don't worry about them, because you will still be able to visit them whenever you want. But you will probably be too busy to visit them literally any time, because the Young Neos are always on the move."

That reassured me, but I still wasn't entirely sure about it. I liked the idea of getting to work with other young heroes—

especially if it meant getting closer to Incantation, who I was sure I could woo if she just let me—but at the same time, I didn't just want to up and leave my parents like that. As annoying as they could be, my parents were my parents and they deserved to know about this, whether or not they approved.

So I said, "Thanks for the offer, Incantation, but I want to talk this over with my parents first. They need to know about it."

Unless my eyes were playing tricks on me, I thought I saw anger flash in Incantation's eyes.

But it was only for a moment and then Incantation nodded and said, "I understand. If you want to contact me with your decision at some point, take this."

Incantation handed me a small, star-shaped device. Taking the device, I looked at it closely and saw that it had two buttons: A blue one and a red one.

Looking up at Incantation, I asked, "What is this?"

"We call it the Star Caller," said Incantation. "Just press one of the buttons and the device will send a message to our headquarters. The red button means that you want to join, while the blue button means that you don't."

"So all I have to do is press one of the buttons and you guys will know whether I accept your offer," I said.

"Exactly," said Incantation. "If you decide to join, we'll send someone to transport you to Hero Island."

I put the Star Caller into the pocket of my suit and said, "All right. Are you going to be in Texas very long?"

"No," said Incantation, shaking her head. "I'm heading back to New York later this afternoon. I've done everything I came here to do. I need to go back home and report to Thaumaturge about what I did here."

"Okay," I said. "But can I have your number? You know, in case the Star Caller fails or something."

Incantation rolled her eyes. She then suddenly twirled her cape around herself, and in a second was gone, like she had just vanished into midair.

"I guess that's a no, then," I said with a sigh.

Deciding that it was time to go, I launched into the sky, wondering what my parents were going to say when I told them about the offer Incantation had made to me. I still wasn't sure if I was going to accept it or not and hoped that maybe Dad would be able to give me some guidance on that.

CHAPTER THREE

SEE, WHENEVER I WANTED to return home, I couldn't just land in our backyard and then walk into the house with my super suit still on in broad daylight. I still had a secret identity to keep, after all, and I didn't want our neighbors to find out who I was.

I couldn't teleport into our house with one of Dad's gadgets, either. True, it would allow me to enter without being seen, but it would also mean that we would have to explain to the neighbors how I could leave the house and then, hours later, leave the house again without any obvious sign of how I returned in the first place. Dad didn't trust me with teleportation anyway, so that method was out regardless.

Instead, I had to fly just a little ways out of town, land in a hilly, uninhabited area that also had a few trees for extra covering, and then take my suit off there. Then I had to walk back to the house, which wasn't that bad, because I still had super speed and would occasionally use it to give me a teeny tiny extra boost of speed. Not enough that anyone would notice me racing through town, but enough so that anyone who saw me would assume that

I am a runner (actually, my PE teacher at school had once seen me running like this and offered me a position on the school's track team, which I declined because I wanted to spend my time practicing my super powers instead of competing in sports).

As I drew closer to my house, decreasing my speed to a more normal speed, I noticed that both of the cars were parked there, which meant that Mom and Dad were home. But there was also a new car in the driveway, a car I had never seen before. It was a dirty, beat-up station wagon, of all things, that looked like it had been driven straight out of a dump. Its windows were cracked; and of the windows that *weren't* cracked, they were covered with cardboard and tape. It looked like the sort of thing a homeless person would drive.

I slowed down to a walk when I reached the driveway. I noticed that the station wagon had a New York license plate, which made me wonder what someone from New York was doing all the way down here in Texas. Did Mom or Dad invite a friend over without telling me? That didn't seem like them, since Mom and Dad didn't usually invite people over to our house, much less without telling me ahead of time, but I couldn't think of any other explanation.

So I entered the house and said, “Mom, Dad? Whose car is parked out in our driveway?”

“Kevin, you're back already,” said Dad, his voice coming from the living room. He didn't sound pleased, which I took as a bad sign. “Why don't you come into the living room and meet our guest?”

Guest? I wondered who it could be. I walked into the living room, albeit somewhat hesitantly, because I worried that Dad's displeased tone wasn't a good sign.

When I entered the living room, I saw two people were in there. One of them was Dad, sitting on the couch, who wore his usual blue button down shirt and black slacks. His arms weren't in casts anymore, having healed up from when Master Chaos broke them last month, but he still moved them slowly and gingerly, likely because they still hurt.

The other guy, however, I didn't recognize at all. He appeared to be Asian and wore a large overcoat that reminded me of a detective. He was very thin, even skinny, but when he looked at me, I could tell he was no pushover. He was reclining in one of the recliners, but he didn't look relaxed. With his shifty, questioning eyes, he seemed to think we were about to be attacked at any moment.

Dad waved at me. “Hi, Kevin. How was Fallsville?”

I was about to answer, but then I noticed Dad's tone. He sounded like he knew *exactly* what happened there, which confirmed my worst fears.

So I said, “Uh, I'll tell you about it later.” I looked at the man sitting in the recliner, who had not uttered a word since I entered. “Um, who's this?”

“An old friend of mine from my superhero days,” said Dad lightly. “His name is Mieko Hiro, but you might know him better as the superhero Triplet.”

I blinked. “Triplet? I don't think I've heard that name before.”

“Few have,” said Triplet in a soft and clear voice. “And I intend to keep it that way.”

It didn't sound like a threat, but the way Triplet said it made me wonder if he was going to pull out a knife and threaten to slit my throat if I told anyone who he was. I stepped away from him, which he seemed to notice immediately, because his eyes followed my feet, though he didn't say anything about it.

"Wait, does he know your secret identity?" I said to Dad.

Dad nodded. "Yes. We used to work together in the Neohero Alliance before I retired."

"I figured it out on my own," said Triplet, causing me to look at him again. "Most neoheroes don't hide their secret identities nearly as well as they think. Just use some basic logic and deduction skills and you can figure out practically any mask's real identity in a few days or even hours if they are particularly careless."

"Does that mean you know who I am?" I said.

"Knew it before I even spoke with Ted," said Triplet, gesturing at Dad. "As I said, most neoheroes are bad at hiding their identities. Especially younger ones like yourself, who tend to overestimate their own cleverness."

Triplet spoke as casually about learning my secret identity as if it was something he did every day. It made me wonder what else he knew about me. I suddenly felt like I had my privacy violated.

"Where's Mom?" I said.

"In the kitchen," said Triplet. He gestured at the kitchen. "I'm in there with her getting some tea."

"Huh?" I said. "No, you're here, sitting on one of our chairs and talking with us."

"Yes, but I am also in the kitchen," Triplet insisted. "I should be coming out with my tea any second now."

Before I could ask Dad if Triplet was a 'special' person (and not in the superhero way), I heard movement from the kitchen and a second later Triplet stepped out of the kitchen and into the living room. It was literally Triplet, down to the same amused facial expression and same old overcoat. The only difference was that he held a steaming teacup in his hand.

The teacup-holding Triplet walked across the living room to the Triplet sitting on the recliner, ignoring my startled looks. The Triplet with the tea placed the teacup on the coffee table and then stood in front of the Triplet sitting on the recliner.

Before my startled eyes, the standing Triplet turned into a glowing blue light before being sucked into the sitting Triplet. The sitting Triplet glowed blue briefly before returning to normal, thus leaving him the sole Triplet in the room.

Then the remaining Triplet leaned forward, picked up the teacup, and started sipping his tea. He took one sip and sighed. "I missed your wife's tea, Ted. It was always better than mine."

I looked at Dad. Like Triplet, Dad didn't even look fazed by what happened. He almost looked bored, even a little annoyed, like he thought Triplet was showing off.

"Um …" I looked from Dad to Triplet and back again. "Huh?"

"Triplet's power," said Dad. "He can split into three clones that can act independently of each other, but share a same mind and must eventually return to the original after five hours or cease existing."

"Ah, not 'clones,' Ted," said Triplet, shaking his head. "I call them 'Thirds.' How many times do I have to correct you on that?"

Dad looked like he wanted to roll his eyes, but didn't because Triplet was a friend. "Right, right, how could I forget your preferred terminology?"

"That's a seriously cool power," I said, looking at Triplet again. "Really freaky and mind-blowing, but cool nonetheless."

"It is helpful in my line of work," said Triplet, taking another sip of his tea. "Sometimes I need to be in three places at once. And unlike most people, I am perfectly capable of doing that."

"What kind of work do you do?" I said.

"Detective work," said Triplet. "I am the owner of Triple Eye Investigation."

"You mean you're a real life private eye?" I said. "Like Sherlock Holmes?"

"In a way, yes," said Triplet. "But I don't have a Watson, nor do I need one. I have everyone I need right here."

Triplet patted his chest and then resumed sipping his tea.

"Before that, however, Triplet was a superhero and member of the NHA, like me," said Dad. "We worked alongside each other for a while until he quit the team eleven years ago. That's how we became friends."

"Why did you quit the NHA?" I said to Triplet. "Did you just want to strike out on your own or something?"

Triplet exchanged a quick but significant look with my Dad before looking at me again. "Let's just say that I had some disagreements with how the organization was run and leave it at that."

That was hardly a satisfying answer to me, but when I saw Dad give me the 'drop-the-subject' look, I didn't press it anymore. Besides, Dad seemed to be in a bad mood already and I didn't want to make it even worse by poking into a subject that was obviously a hot topic for both of them.

Instead, I said, "Why did you come here all the way from New York? Just to say hi to Dad? That seems like an awful long drive, especially in that old beat-up station wagon."

I could immediately tell that Triplet was deciding how much information to share with me. I could tell because he had a very similar look on his face to how Dad looked whenever he was deciding the same thing.

Finally, Triplet said, "I am investigating something for a client of mine and the trail of clues has led me all the way out here. I'm supposed to be in Fallsville, really, but I decided to stop by Silvers just to say hi to your father and catch up on old times for a bit before I head there."

"You can't tell me what you're investigating?" I said.

"I never reveal the identities of my clients or what I am investigating to people who have nothing to do with the case," said Triplet. "In other words, it's none of your business."

I couldn't argue with that, so I said, "How long are you going to be in town?"

"Not sure," said Triplet. "And even if I did know, I wouldn't let you know, because, again, it's none of your business."

I nodded, but I had to admit I was very curious about what it was. I didn't think there was anything out here in Texas that could possibly interest a detective like him, but I guess Triplet knew something I didn't.

Then Triplet finished his tea and said, "All right. Well, it was nice catching up on old times, Ted, and thanks for the teleportation disks. And a pleasure meeting your son, too. But I have to leave for Fallsville before it gets too dark, so if you will excuse me, I have to leave."

"Sure," said Dad. "Feel free to drop by whenever you like. Will you be staying for dinner?"

Triplet put his teacup on the coffee table and stood up. "No. Likely I'll be spending the night in my station wagon eating some grub from some fast food joint in Fallsville."

"Can't you get a hotel room, at least?" said Dad.

Triplet shook his head. "I don't trust hotels."

I was about to ask him why, but then he walked past me and was out the door in an instant. Then I heard the car rumble to life and leave until soon I could no longer hear it. It all happened so fast that I wasn't sure it even happened at first, despite the teacup on the coffee table.

I looked at Dad. "Um … has Triplet always been that way? And what did he mean about 'teleportation disks'?"

"For as long as I've known him," said Dad with a shrug. "He's always been strange, even by neohero standards, so I wouldn't worry about it. As for the disks, they're just something I've been toying with and which I gave to him as a gift from an old friend."

"Uh, right," I said. I shifted my weight, not meeting Dad's gaze. "Well, I think I'll just go to my room now and—"

"I saw you on TV."

Oh, boy. I knew *that* tone. It wasn't exactly angry; more disappointed. I just scratched the back of my neck, still not meeting Dad's gaze. I could feel his eyes on me, though, eyes that seemed to be looking right through me.

"Oh, you did?" I said. "Was I caught on camera or something while I was walking down the street like an innocent bystander?"

"Kevin, stop playing dumb," said Dad. He gestured at the TV, which was off. "I saw the news report about Steel Skin's attack on the Plutarch rally. I also saw you and Incantation fighting him."

I bit my lower lip. "Huh, I didn't know we were being filmed. I thought the reporters had run away when Steel Skin attacked."

"Kevin, what did I say about performing superheroics?" said Dad. "How many times have I told you that you should not be fighting supervillains and criminals until you graduate from high school?"

"I know, I know, but Steel Skin robbed a bank and I—"

"Should have left that to the G-Men or NHA," Dad finished. "You were only supposed to go to Fallsville to get a car, not get into a fight with a supervillain."

"But Dad, if I didn't do that, then he would have killed Plutarch," I said. "And probably other people at the rally, too. It would have been a mess."

"Plutarch would have had it coming, considering everything he's said and done," said Dad.

I actually looked at Dad in shock when he said that. "But Plutarch is a civilian! I know he was a supervillain at one point, but he hasn't done anything bad for years, so killing him wouldn't be justified."

"A leopard never changes its spots," said Dad, shaking his head. "Regardless, it was still not your responsibility to stop Steel Skin and you knew that."

"Yeah, I know," I said. "But I still did the right thing, didn't I? I stopped him. Well, really Incantation did, but—"

"And what was Incantation doing there?" said Dad.

"You know her?" I said in surprise.

"I met her when she was a young girl, before she got her powers," said Dad. "I know her uncle, Thaumaturge, from the

NHA."

I should have felt surprised, but it seemed like Dad knew everyone in the neohero community, so I just accepted it.

"Well, Incantation wanted to talk with me," I said. "She offered me a position on the Young Neos."

Dad raised an eyebrow. "The Young Neos?"

"Yeah," I said, nodding. "She and the other Young Neos saw the livestream of my fight with Master Chaos last month. She thought I would make a great member of the team."

"Did you accept her offer?" said Dad.

I shook my head. "Not yet. I told her I wanted to tell you and Mom about this first."

"Tell us about what now?" said Mom, stepping out of the kitchen wearing her apron.

"About the offer I was given to join the Young Neos," I said. "They're a superhero team made up of young heroes like myself. They're under the supervision of Thaumaturge, one of the NHA leaders."

"I've never heard of them before," said Mom. She squeezed her hands together. "Do they fight crime and villains like adult neoheroes?"

"Pretty much, although not to the same extent, from what I understand," I said. "But anyway, I really want to join. It's a great opportunity for me to advance in my superhero career."

"You mean the superhero career that we don't want you to have?" said Dad.

I folded my arms across my chest. "Come on, Dad. This could be a great opportunity for me to learn how to control my powers better. Besides, it isn't like we'll be unsupervised, since

Thaumaturge oversees it. Not only that, but I won't have to miss my education, because they have tutors for each member of the team."

"I am aware of the benefits offered to members of the Young Neos, since I was there when the first version of the team was formed," said Dad. He adjusted his glasses. "I thought it was a foolish idea for a team back then and I still think it is one now."

"What?" I said. "Why?"

"Because I don't think teenagers or kids should be encouraged to fight crime and villains like this," said Dad. "It's dangerous. And most of these teens don't really fully understand how dangerous being a superhero really is. If I had my way, it wouldn't exist at all."

"But didn't you start your superhero career when you were eleven?" I said. "I think you turned out pretty well for it, didn't you?"

Dad rubbed his forehead and didn't look at me. "Just because I did something does not mean I want you to go through the same thing."

"I have to agree with your father," said Mom. "Being a neohero is already dangerous even if you are an adult. Putting kids in the kinds of situations that even most adults can't handle is, in my opinion, extremely irresponsible."

"Your mother is correct," said Dad, nodding. "Kevin, I know how exciting the Young Neos seem, but I can't let you join them, not while you still live in my house, anyway."

I frowned. "So that's a no, then?"

"Exactly," said Dad. "And there will be no debate on the subject, either. I want you to focus on two things at the moment:

Finishing school and getting your car so you can go to college next year."

I looked to Mom for help, but I could tell that she agreed with Dad on this. I was about to resume arguing with Dad anyway, but then I realized that Dad was not going to budge, nor would Mom. Besides, I was feeling sore after my fight with Steel Skin earlier and just wanted to rest more than anything right now.

So I sighed and said, "All right. I'll let Incantation know that I won't accept her offer, then."

"Good," said Dad, his tone becoming a lot more positive now. "You've made a wise decision, Kevin."

I nodded, though without any enthusiasm. "Yeah, okay. I'm going to my room now to rest a bit before dinner."

With that, I went to my room, closed the door behind me, and lay down on my bed. But I didn't go to sleep just yet. I pulled out the Star Caller from my pocket, the device Incantation had given me that I could use to contact her with my answer. My thumb hovered over the blue button, the one that would let her know that I wasn't going to join the team, but then I hesitated. If I rejected her offer now, would I ever get a chance like this again?

The answer to that question was obvious. So, instead of pressing the blue button, I got up, pulled open the top drawer of my desk, and dropped the Star Caller inside it. I stared at the device for a moment, wondering if I should just press the red button anyway, but then closed the drawer.

Before I made any permanent decisions, I needed to talk about this with someone who wasn't my parents. And I knew exactly who.

CHAPTER FOUR

"SO YOU WERE OFFERED a position on the Young Neos by Incantation herself?" said Malcolm, staring at me in shock. "Get out of here."

"No, I'm telling the truth," I said. "You saw our fight with Steel Skin on the news yesterday, didn't you?"

Malcolm and I sat on the front steps of John Smith High School, which was the school I attended. It was Monday and we were having lunch together outside today, instead of at our usual spot in the cafeteria. That was because I wanted to avoid being overheard by the other students or faculty, and because most of them ate lunch in the cafeteria, this was the most logical place in the school to talk in private. There were a few other students nearby, sitting underneath the trees or at some of the picnic tables, but they were far enough away that they couldn't hear us. Besides, the other students were too absorbed in their own conversations or smartphones to notice us and we weren't speaking very loudly, so I felt pretty safe.

"Yeah, I saw the fight at the Plutarch rally, but the news didn't show what happened to you after it," said Malcolm. "So you just went off together and talked?"

"Pretty much," I said. "She said she came all the way out to Texas just to talk with me."

"That's pretty amazing," said Malcolm. "She must really like you or something."

Malcolm sounded more than a little jealous, prompting me to say, "Oh, I asked her out, but she rejected me, so I doubt she has any, like, real interest in me or anything. She probably just thought I could be a good member of the team. Nothing romantic."

Malcolm suddenly looked a lot less jealous. "Yeah, I guess. So what did you say? Did you accept?"

"I told her I wanted to talk about it with my parents first," I said.

"And what did your parents say?" said Malcolm.

"A big, fat no," I said with a sigh. "You know what my dad's opinion about superheroics is."

"Bummer, man," said Malcolm. "The Young Neos are awesome. Even though they're all really young, they all have really high rankings on Neo Ranks. Incantation is a six, which is pretty high for a younger hero."

"I know," I said, shaking my head. Then I paused. "Wait, she's just a six? I'm a seven."

"Yeah, but that's because you beat Master Chaos," said Malcolm. "Incantation hasn't fought any major villains like that, at least not that I know of. She's most well-known for helping to defeat Mirakill, but Mirakill is a six, too, so he's not on Master Chaos or Nuclear Winter's level."

"That must be why she wanted me on the team," I said. "I'm

already higher than her. She'd probably raise the profile of the team quite a bit if she had me on it."

"Yeah, but who cares?" said Malcolm. "If you joined the Young Neos, it would open even more opportunities for you as a superhero."

"Assuming my parents will even let me," I said with a sigh. "They were pretty adamant about not letting me join yesterday."

"That sucks," said Malcolm.

"But," I said, "I didn't throw out the device Incantation gave me, the one I could use to contact her and let her know my decision. It's back home in the drawer of my desk."

"Why are you keeping it if you aren't allowed to join them?" said Malcolm. "Are you planning to join them anyway, regardless of what your parents say?"

I shrugged. "Well, I mean, I'm almost an adult now. I don't think I need my parents' approval for every little thing. I still haven't gotten back to Incantation about this yet, but that's why I wanted to talk with you. I wanted to get your opinion on it."

"Well, my opinion is that you should run back home right now, grab that device, and let Incantation know that you want to be on the team," said Malcolm. "I wouldn't waste even another second talking to me if I were you. You never know how long this offer is going to last, after all. What if you take too long to get back to her and Incantation decides you aren't interested and looks for someone else?"

"I never thought of that," I said. "I thought the offer would always stand."

"Eh, I wouldn't be so sure about that," said Malcolm. "At least if I were her, I wouldn't waste my time waiting for someone to respond to my very generous offer."

"Good point," I said. "Maybe when I get home, I'll contact Incantation and talk to her about this. I'm just worried about what my parents will think."

"They'll be fine, I'm sure," said Malcolm. "Just because they think it's a bad idea now doesn't mean they always will. I'm sure they'll come around to it."

Malcolm seemed too optimistic about my parents, but then again, he didn't know them nearly as well as I. He didn't know how serious my parents were about ensuring I didn't make superheroics my career. Still, I really wanted to join the Young Neos and so was really tempted to just use the Star Caller as soon as I went home after school today.

Then, all of a sudden, loud laughter came out of nowhere, startling me and Malcolm. I looked around, wondering where the laughter was coming from until I noticed a few students sitting under one of the trees nearby. I didn't recognize most of them, but I did recognize the large, tanned skin blond-haired guy sitting in the middle of them: It was Robert Candle, the son of Bernard Candle, also known as Master Chaos.

Robert Candle was the local bully of John Smith High School, who tried to give me trouble when I first got here but ended up getting punched through the cafeteria wall by yours truly (accidentally, of course). He had helped Master Chaos try to kill me and had just recently gotten off his crutches, though he didn't participate in sports anymore due to the fact that he was still recovering from his injuries.

The two of us were basically archenemies, although we had not gotten into any conflicts with each other since he got out of the hospital. That was mostly, I think, due to the fact that he was a normal human and I was not, so he didn't want to get punched through a wall again. He still glared at me, though, whenever no one was looking, and I'd glare right back, which was about as close to coming to blows as we'd come since he returned to school.

I thought that Robert and his friends had laughed at something I said, but then I noticed that they were all watching a video on Robert's smartphone. I couldn't see what it was from here, but the volume was loud enough for me to make out a loud, angry voice with a familiar New York accent. But it was hard to identify who was speaking because Robert and his friends would break out into riotous laughter every few minutes, sometimes even giving each other high fives. None of them seemed to notice me or Malcolm.

"What are they laughing at?" I said, tilting my head to the side.

Malcolm frowned and actually glared at Robert, which surprised me, because Malcolm was usually too timid to even look at Robert, despite knowing that I could protect him if Robert ever tried to bully him. "Probably one of Plutarch's speeches."

"Plutarch?" I said. "You mean Adam Plutarch? The guy who is running for President?"

"Yeah," said Malcolm. He punched his fist into his other hand. "Sometimes I just want to punch that idiot in the face."

"I didn't know Robert was a Plutarch fan," I said, glancing at Robert and his friends again. "I thought Robert was too stupid to follow politics."

"He's stupid enough for Plutarch," said Malcolm. "But I can guess why he likes him: Plutarch hates neoheroes."

"He does?" I said.

"Yeah," said Malcolm. He looked at me in surprise. "Haven't you been watching his speeches? He's on the news all the time, talking about 'making America normal again' and crap like that."

Malcolm did air quotes around the phrase 'making America normal again' when he said it, like he didn't actually agree with it.

"I'm just not very interested in politics," I admitted. "So I don't really know what Plutarch's opinions or positions are."

"You're lucky," said Malcolm. "Plutarch keeps saying things like neoheroes can't be trusted, that they're just a problem that needs to be dealt with. He said he's going to force neoheroes to pay for all of the collateral damage that they cause in their fights. He's a lunatic."

"He seemed pretty sane when I spoke with him," I said.

"You've met him?" said Malcolm. "When?"

"After Incantation and I saved him," I said. "He talked to me briefly and even gave me his card in case I wanted to talk with him."

"While you were in full costume?" said Malcolm in astonishment. "That's weird."

"I know," I said with a shrug. "He was just grateful that Incantation and I saved him, though he looked at Incantation like she had insulted him."

"No surprise there," said Malcolm with a snort. "Plutarch has a Neo Ranks page as the Billionaire. He made a lot of enemies in the neohero community before retiring, including Thaumaturge, Incantation's master."

"Yeah, my Dad doesn't like him, either," I said. "I just wonder how he managed to become so popular if he's so stupid."

"Because he *isn't* stupid," said a voice behind us, causing Malcolm and I to look over our shoulders.

Standing in the doorway to the school was Tara Reynolds. Unusually, her face wasn't buried in her smartphone at the moment. She stood with her hand keeping the door open, looking down at us from behind her glasses. She looked as cute as ever, even if she was looking at Malcolm in annoyance.

"Tara, what are you doing out here?" Malcolm. "How long have you been standing there?"

"Just a few seconds," said Tara. "I only heard the last thing Kevin said about Plutarch. I came out here because I got tired of the noise of the cafeteria and wanted a little peace and quiet."

I was hugely relieved that Tara had only heard that last bit, because I worried that she had overheard us talking about the Young Neos and my fight with Steel Skin. Unlike Malcolm, Tara didn't know about my secret identity, as I had not yet told her about it, and wasn't sure if I ever would due to the fact that she was pretty anti-neohero herself.

"What do you mean that Plutarch isn't stupid?" said Malcolm. "Come on. Have you heard the guy talk? He's insane. I mean, he's a former supervillain, for Pete's sake."

"Yeah, *former*," said Tara, closing the door behind her and walking over to us. "He's an honest businessman now. And anyway, it doesn't change the fact that his views on neoheroes are right."

"No, they're not," said Malcolm, shaking his head. "He's just letting his own negative experiences with them in the past color his views. He doesn't know what he's talking about half the time."

Tara rolled her eyes. "And your friend Barney does?"

"Barney?" I said, looking between Malcolm and Tara in confusion. "Is Barney the Dinosaur running for President now?"

"She's talking about Barnabas Sagan," said Malcolm, who seemed annoyed at Tara's nickname for Sagan. "He's Plutarch's rival in the election, the candidate for the other party."

"What's so great about him?" I said.

"Unlike Plutarch, Sagan was never a supervillain," said Malcolm. "He's a Senator from some northeastern state, been in the Senate for years. He's nowhere near as rich as Plutarch, but if you ask me, he's a lot more honest and much friendlier to neoheroes than Plutarch could ever be."

"Because he's an old loon who has a rosy-eyed view of superhumans," Tara said, shaking her head. "His home state doesn't have as many neoheroes as others, which is probably why he doesn't see them as the threat they are."

"You're wrong," said Malcolm, standing up and staring Tara in the eye. "He knows more about neoheroes than Plutarch. He just knows that they are our friends and we shouldn't burden them with unnecessary fees."

"You mean force them to take responsibility for their actions?" said Tara, not backing down. "Are you telling me that the powerful shouldn't be held accountable when they destroy things?"

"I'm saying that neoheroes shouldn't be taxed out of existence," said Malcolm. "Because that's what Plutarch wants to do. He just wants to bankrupt the NHA and the INJ and every other neohero organization out there so that the G-Men are the only functioning neohero organization in the country. He wants the government to have more control over the superhuman community."

Tara looked like she was about to start yelling at Malcolm, so I stood up and, raising my hands, said, "Hey, guys, we don't need to fight about this. It's just politics, I mean, we're not even old enough to vote yet. Who cares whether you support Plutarch or Sagan or someone else?"

"Stay out of this, Kevin," said Tara. "You don't know anything, so your opinions just come across as ignorant."

"Ignorant?" said Malcolm. "Is that what we're doing now? Insulting each other because we don't meet *your* arbitrary standards of informativeness?"

"Guys," I said, "this really isn't a big deal. I'm not offended or anything. I'm just saying that we should all just calm down and be friends. Isn't that what we are?"

For a moment, I feared that Malcolm and Tara really were going to fight. I mean, I could stop them pretty easily with only the slightest application of my powers if I had to, but I really didn't want to.

Then Tara shook her head and said, "Lunch is almost over. I'm heading to class now. Bye."

With that, Tara turned away and marched right back into the school. She yanked the door open and stomped inside without even looking over her shoulder at us.

I looked at Malcolm, who didn't look very happy at the moment. "Are you all right, Mal?"

"I'm fine," said Malcolm. "Tara is just being her usual obnoxious self. I'm going back to class, too."

Malcolm lifted his backpack off the steps and went back into the school without even waiting for me to go with him. I just stood there, unsure if I had just witnessed the end of a friendship. I hoped I hadn't.

CHAPTER FIVE

MALCOLM AND TARA DIDN'T talk to each other for the rest of the school day after that, even when they sat next to each other in class. They didn't even acknowledge each other's existence. I tried to stay friendly with both of them, but it didn't seem to help. I knew politics could divide people, but it was really hard seeing my two best friends act this way because of some petty political disagreement. I hoped it wouldn't last for long. I bet that by the end of the week, they'd be friendly to each other again.

How wrong was I. By the end of the week, Malcolm and Tara were still as hostile toward each other as they had been on Monday. And I really didn't know how to mediate between them, because I didn't know much about politics or how to solve political disagreements. I just tried to avoid the topic whenever I hung out with them, though the tension in the air was always so thick that I could practically taste it.

So I tried to focus on other things, like Incantation's offer. Even though Malcolm had convinced me to accept it, I didn't want to go to New York right away. If I activated the Star Caller and was whisked away to the Young Neos' headquarters in New York, my parents would notice my absence and probably come straight to New York to haul me back. Then Dad would probably invent some kind of machine to take away my powers or maybe construct a bunker made out of titanium to keep me from ever leaving the house again or something like that.

Therefore, my plan was simple: Wait until the weekend, then tell Mom and Dad that I was going to spend the weekend at Malcolm's house and would be back by Sunday night. Of course, what I really intended to do was contact the Young Neos and have them take me to their headquarters so I could see it. I even told Malcolm about it, just in case my parents contacted him or saw him over the weekend for some reason.

Thus, when Saturday finally came, I said good bye to my parents, left the house, and walked in the general direction of Malcolm's house for a couple of miles. Once I was safely out of the sight of my house, I quickly changed course, heading for an abandoned lot that I had discovered on my way to school one time when I was looking for a shortcut. As far as I knew, no one ever came over to this lot, which meant that I would be able to suit up without being seen. It was early morning, too, so most people weren't awake just yet.

Once I got to the lot, I pressed the button on my suit-up watch and soon was in my full superhero costume. Then I pulled the Star Caller out of my pocket and was just about to press the red button when a voice in my ear said, "Bolt? What are you doing?"

I paused in fear. "Valerie? What are you doing here?"

"Well, I am connected to your earcom, so I'm always with you wherever you go," said Valerie. "But why are you in your super suit? Did you not tell your parents that you were going to be staying at Malcolm's house over the weekend?"

Damn it. I had forgotten about Valerie. My earcom was so small and unobtrusive that I sometimes forgot that it was there. But I couldn't just remove it now, not when Valerie was aware of what I was doing.

"Well ..." I tried to think of a good excuse, but it was hard because panic was starting to take over. "Um, I was actually thinking of flying to Malcolm's house."

"In your super suit?" said Valerie. "I know that Malcolm knows of your secret identity, but I assume that the rest of his family does not. If you fly there, though, then they will see you and know who you are."

"Yeah, but, um ..." I looked around hurriedly, trying to think of a good explanation. "Well, actually, I'm not going to fly to Malcolm's house at all. Instead, I am going to, er—"

"Is that the Star Caller in your hand?" said Valerie. "The device Incantation gave you after you spoke with her last week?"

I knew Valerie was an AI and therefore not very easy to fool, but I still cursed under my breath when I realized that she noticed the Star Caller.

Because it was obvious that I couldn't keep lying, I said, "All right, Val. I'm not going to Malcolm's house. That was a lie. I'm actually going to contact the Young Neos and go to their base on Hero Island instead."

"Why?" said Valerie. "I understand that Genius forbid you from joining the Young Neos."

"I don't really want to *join* them, per se," I said. "Just meet their members, check out their base, and see what they do and stuff like that."

That was a flat-out lie, but I hoped that Valerie wouldn't notice.

"But why did you have to lie to your parents about your true intentions, then?" said Valerie. "Why shouldn't I contact Genius and inform him of your deception before you leave?"

Because then I'd get into trouble, but I knew that line of reasoning wouldn't work with Valerie, so instead I said, "Because Dad doesn't really need to know this. I mean, it's not like I'm going after some powerful supervillain or whatever. I'm just going to go and visit Hero Island for a while. I'll be perfectly safe."

"Genius would not be pleased if he found out that I hid your real location from him," said Valerie.

"Well, you don't *really* need to 'hide' it, per se," I said. "Just don't say anything if Dad asks you about me."

"You want me to lie to my creator?" said Valerie.

"Not lying," I said, shaking my head. "Just, well, not mentioning the facts. That doesn't count as lying, does it?"

"Technically, I guess it doesn't," said Valerie. "But I still do not like it."

"You don't have to," I said. "You just need to do it, okay? I mean, you've helped me in the past, haven't you?"

"Yes, but my helping you has gotten me into trouble with Genius," said Valerie. "I can't say I have benefited from being your secret keeper."

"Well, how's about you keep my secret just this once and I will never ask you to do this for me again?" I said. "Doesn't that sound reasonable?"

"I suppose," said Valerie. "But just this once."

"Great," I said. "Knew I could count on you, Val. So just sit tight while I contact the Young Neos."

Valerie went silent, but I could tell she was having some doubts about this. I knew, however, she would not go against her word, because she was very honest due to being programmed that way by Dad.

So I pressed the red button on the Star Caller. The button glowed a bright red for only a second before I removed my thumb, causing the glow to fade.

I didn't know how long I'd have to wait for a response, but apparently it wasn't for long, because a second later a dimensional portal opened up in front of me and someone walked out.

The guy who stood before me was about my age, maybe a year younger, with long dreads and dark skin. He wore a super suit that looked similar to mine, except it was green and yellow instead of red and black, and he wore a mask that looked like mine, except without the goggles. He also had a symbol on his right shoulder, a picture of a cartoon superhero flying, which I assumed was the symbol of the Young Neos.

"Hey there," said the guy in a very friendly voice. He held out a hand. "You're Bolt, right? I'm Hopper."

I shook the guy's hand and found that he had a surprisingly strong grip, even though he seemed very thin. "Hopper? Is that your real name?"

"Nope," said Hopper, shaking his head. "It's my superhero name. It's a reference to my powers." He gestured at the portal behind him. "I can hop across the world with these portals, hence the name."

"Cool," I said. I frowned. "But you answered the Star Caller rather fast."

"Well, Incantation told me that you might be contacting us soon, so I've just been waiting for your response all week," said Hopper. "Besides, I've always wanted to meet the guy who beat Master Chaos, so when you called, I didn't waste any time leaving the House."

I scratched the back of my head in embarrassment. "Well, it's not that big of a deal."

"Not that big a deal?" said Hopper. "Dude, Master Chaos gave even Omega Man trouble back in the day. Even Incantation has never beaten a villain on his level before. You should be proud of yourself."

"Well, I guess you have a point," I said. "So how are we going to get to Hero Island?"

Hopper thrust a thumb over his shoulder at the portal behind him. "We can get there using my portal. Follow me."

Hopper turned and walked into the portal. I looked around one last time, just to make sure that no one was watching, and then walked into the portal after Hopper.

Having never walked through a portal before, I expected to find myself walking through some weird, technicolor void of despair that would make me think I'd gone on a trip.

Instead, it was actually like walking through a normal doorway. I simply stepped through the portal and found myself standing inside the hallway of what looked like a futuristic spaceship. There was no real transition between Texas and New York at all; in fact, the change in scenery was so abrupt that I thought that maybe I was hallucinating before I heard the portal close behind me with a tiny *pop*.

"Here we are," said Hopper, spreading his arms to indicate our surroundings. "Welcome to the House, the base and headquarters of the Young Neos, located on Hero Island, New York."

I looked around the hall. It was fairly large, like it was designed to allow large groups of people to walk around in. The walls, floor, and ceiling were covered with orange metal panels that were sparklingly clean, so clean that I felt dirty just looking at them, even though my suit was clean and I had taken a shower before leaving home. The hallway stretched out of sight, which gave the impression to me that the House was huge.

"Wow," I said, looking around the hallway, impressed. "This looks like something straight out of a sci-fi movie or something."

"It isn't just pretty," said Hopper. He tapped the floor with his foot. "Made out of the strongest metal in the world. It can even withstand a nuclear blast."

"Really?" I said in surprise. "Why is it so strong?"

Hopper looked at me like I had just asked a dumb question. "We're a bunch of hormonal teenagers with superpowers. You do the math."

I nodded. "Right. So where is everyone else?"

"In the meeting room," said Hopper. "Come on. I'll take you there."

"Can't you just open a portal to take us there directly?" I said.

Hopper shook his head. "Nope. Incantation said I'm not supposed to use my portals in the meeting room. It's against House rules."

"Why?" I said.

Hopper brushed back some of his dreads. "See, I can't just open my portals in a small, enclosed space like that. If I do, the portal has a habit of turning into a void that sucks people directly into it and drops them off in the most random—and hilarious—places imaginable."

"Why?" I said. "Don't you have control over your powers?"

Hopper turned his hands into fists. "I do, but it's just a natural reaction. My portals work best in wide-open places, like that lot we were just in, or in larger enclosed areas like the hall. But turning it into a void can be useful in a fight. Just ask Seaweed."

"Who?"

"Exactly," said Hopper. "Anyway, come on. The others are waiting and they're all really impatient."

Hopper immediately started walking down the hall. I followed him, but could not keep my eyes from wandering. I wondered what kind of security systems that the hall might have. I expected lasers or robots to come out of the walls and try to attack me, even though there was no reason for them to do that. This reminded me of Dad's inventions, but I quickly stopped thinking about that because I started feeling guilty whenever I thought about my parents, who didn't know I was here.

We soon came upon a set of doors that slid into the walls Star Trek style, which we walked through. When we passed through the open doorway, the doors closed behind us and I looked around at the room we had entered.

Hopper and I stood in a room that was somewhat open, but much less so than the hallway outside. Comfy sofas, chairs, and beanbags were scattered here and there, though most of them were set before the gigantic flat screen TV on the other end of the wall, which was currently off. I saw what looked like all of the newest video game consoles—plus dozens of controllers—underneath the TV, which meant that this was also their video game room. It was an awesome set up and I wondered if I'd get a chance to try it out while I was here.

In the center of the room was a large, round table that appeared to be made out of black marble. Four people sat around the table and looked like they had been in the middle of a discussion, but had stopped talking when we entered the room.

I recognized the first one right away: Incantation. She had ditched her robes, but still wore her cape, and she looked as beautiful as ever. She sat at the head of the table, in between the other three, probably because she was the leader.

To her right sat a bald guy who I could see through—Literally. He was totally transparent; in fact, he was so transparent that I wondered how he had not just fallen through the floor already. Maybe he was really floating and only appeared to be sitting.

And to Incantation's left was a girl who had a mechanical right arm. She was taller than Incantation and looked very much like an athlete. She wasn't nearly as pretty as Incantation, but she was good-looking, I thought, and she could probably handle herself pretty well in a fight, though I couldn't guess what her powers were.

Then there was the fourth and final person, another girl. She seemed to be slightly younger than the others—maybe fifteen – and wore an ordinary pink tank top and jeans. Her hair was a weird green color; at least, if you could call the thing on her head 'hair,' because it was shaved so low that she looked nearly as bald as the transparent guy.

The girl seemed fearful, because she had her hands folded over her lap and was leaning slightly away from the others. While the others looked at me without any shyness, the girl seemed to shrink back when she saw me. I didn't know why, nor did I know what her powers were. She didn't even wear a super suit, which made me wonder if she was even a member of the team or not.

"Hi, Bolt," said Incantation, waving at me. "I'm glad you decided to join us. Why don't you sit down on one of the free seats and we can talk about your spot on the team?"

"Oh, I'm not ready to join the team just yet," I said as Hopper and I walked over to the table. Hopper took a seat next to the transparent guy, while I sat down on the end of the table directly opposite Incantation. "I just came to meet the team and see what the House is like."

A brief look of annoyance crossed Incantation's features, but then she said, "Oh, that's fine. I understand. Joining the Young Neos, after all, is a big commitment. And I'm sure that by the end of the day, you'll be more than eager to join us."

I nodded, but then noticed the strange girl looking at me. But when I glanced at her, she was looking away, although I thought I saw an angry scowl slowly crossing her features. Maybe I reminded her of someone she knew or maybe her annoyance had nothing to do with me.

"Anyway, let me introduce you to the team," said Incantation. "You already know who Hopper and I are, of course. I'm the leader, while Hopper is my deputy. Just so you are clear on the hierarchy here."

I nodded again and noticed the weird-looking girl make an

ugly face when Incantation mentioned the word 'hierarchy.' Maybe the girl was just jealous that she wasn't the leader.

"This is Ghost," said Incantation, pointing at the transparent guy. "He has the ability to turn transparent and intangible. He can even float."

"Just like a ghost," said the transparent guy, who sounded laid back and relaxed. He smiled. "Nice to meet you, Bolt. I saw your fight with Steel Skin at the Plutarch rally. Really cool, even if Plutarch is a jerk."

"Thanks," I said.

Then Incantation pointed at the athletic girl sitting next to her. "This is Technical. She's our resident mechanic and tech genius and also our best athlete."

"Hello," said Technical, waving at me. "I hope you enjoy the House. We have race tracks, weight rooms, and other places where you can work out, if that's what you're into, plus a workshop for working on technology. We also have a general Training Room, too, for practicing your superpowers."

"Sounds like I know where I'm going first after this meeting," I said.

Technical nodded and then leaned forward and looked at me eagerly. "By the way, your dad is Genius, right?"

"Um, yes," I said. "Why?"

Technical seemed to be trying to restrain herself. "Can I … do you think you can introduce me to him? I've studied his inventions and discoveries and they are amazing. Even the stuff he made when he was a kid is revolutionary. I could learn so much from him. Please?"

I didn't want to tell her that Dad didn't even know I was here, but she looked so cute that I found it impossible to say no. So I said, "Yeah, sure, I can do that, but maybe some other time. I'm sure my dad would be happy to meet a fan."

Technical practically squeed when I said that. "Thank you, thank you! I can't wait."

It was hard not to feel excited with her, but I also felt really strange, because I hadn't known that Dad had fan girls. It made sense, of course, because Dad was a popular superhero in his day, but I wondered what Mom would say if she knew about this.

It looked like Incantation had introduced me to pretty much everyone except for the mystery girl, but I was in a good mood due to how nice they all were, so I looked at her and said, "All right, what's your name, then? What kind of powers do you have?"

My tone was friendly and light, but then she gasped and immediately started sobbing into her hands. Technical draped an arm over the girl's shoulder immediately, while the other Young Neos glared at me like I had just said the most offensive thing in the universe.

"There, there, Sarah, it will be all right," said Technical, her tone soothing. "That insensitive jerk won't hurt you. It will be all right."

"Huh?" I said, looking around, feeling embarrassment creep up my neck even though I wasn't sure what I was supposed to be embarrassed about. "What? What did I say? I just wanted to know her name."

"Bolt," said Ghost. He sounded serious now, not nearly as relaxed or laid back as I initially pegged him. "You asked Sarah what her powers are. That's extremely insensitive." He looked at

Incantation. "And you want this jerk on the team?"

"Hey, I didn't know he was a jerk," said Incantation. Then she glared at me. "Then again, when I saw how buddy buddy Plutarch treated him, maybe I should have realized just what kind of person he really is."

I was so confused right now. I didn't think I'd done anything wrong, but everyone was looking at me like I had just kicked a puppy. I thought about getting up and leaving, but since I didn't want to get lost in the House, I just sat there, wondering if maybe everyone in here was on some kind of drug or something.

"Hey, uh," I said, scratching the back of my head again, "er, I'm not sure what I did wrong."

"Yes, you are!" the girl wailed at me before going back to sobbing. "And it doesn't even matter, because your words are hurtful anyway!"

"No, I genuinely do not understand what I did wrong," I said. I looked at the others for help. "Can anybody help me? Incantation?"

Incantation looked like she was about to order me to leave the room, but then she sighed and said, "Okay. While I normally am not one to forgive such obvious and flagrant insensitivity to our teammates, I can let it pass just this once, seeing as you are new and obviously don't know about Sarah."

"What, does Sarah have some sort of problem or—"

I didn't get to finish the sentence because Hopper suddenly was next to me. He grabbed me by the throat with surprising strength, glaring at me through the slits in his mask.

"Don't say Sarah has a 'problem,' you jerk," said Hopper. He no longer seemed as friendly as he had before; now he seemed like the devil himself. “Remember what I said about creating voids.”

Okay, I wasn't going to put up with this. I grabbed Hopper's arm and ripped it off my throat, causing Hopper to stagger backwards. I was going to stand up and fight him when Incantation said, “Bolt, Hopper! Sit down, both of you. If you fight, you'll just upset Sarah even more.”

I looked at Sarah. She wasn't sobbing quite as hard anymore and actually seemed to have calmed down a little, but she still wouldn't look at me. It was like she was afraid that if she looked at me she'd catch some sort of terrible disease.

I was still angry, angry enough to take on the entire team, but I knew I'd get into trouble with the NHA—and, more importantly, my parents—if I did that. So I stayed where I was, seething in anger, while Hopper returned to his seat next to Ghost.

“Now,” said Incantation, who was still looking at me like I was garbage, “let's have a nice talk about our final—though by no means least important—team member, Sarah Jane Watson.”

I glanced at Sarah, who was sniffling now. Technical kept her arm draped around Sarah's shoulder, like she was going to protect her from me, even though I had no desire whatsoever to even touch her.

“So …” I thought very carefully about how I should phrase this question, because I wasn't interested in being torn apart by the hyenas again. “Does she have a superhero name?”

Sarah looked like she was about to cry again, but Technical said something soothing to her in a low voice. Sarah relaxed slightly.

“No,” said Incantation. “In fact, Sarah doesn't have any

powers whatsoever."

I raised an eyebrow. "No powers at all? Then what's she doing on a team for young neoheroes?"

"Are you saying she doesn't deserve to be on this team any more than you do?" said Ghost, leaning forward and glaring at me. "Huh? Is that what you're saying? That you're *better* than her? Huh?"

I was about to snap back at him, but then Incantation glared at Ghost and he sat back, though he still looked offended for Sarah nonetheless.

"What Ghost was trying to say is that we are an *inclusive* team," said Incantation, looking at me again. "We don't discriminate. Our motto is that you don't need powers to be a hero."

"Well, I guess it's true that you can be a hero without powers," I said. "Police cops and firefighters and soldiers and even ordinary people prove that all the time. But this is a team for young, up-and-coming neoheroes. I'd think that the bare minimum requirement for team membership would be, well, that you have a power of some sort, even if it isn't the fanciest or coolest power in the world."

Technical giggled. "But Sarah *is* a neohero. She identifies as one, after all. And we respect the rights of people to identify however they wish. That's what being a neohero is all about."

"What?" I said. "No, that's not. While no one knows the exact cause of neohero powers, we know they are biological. You can't just call yourself a neohero and somehow become one just through sheer thought alone."

Incantation rolled her eyes. "Oh, so you believe in *that* old theory, do you? Get with the times. Super powers are a social construct, no more objectively real than the laws of the land."

"As long as you *feel* like a neohero, then you are one, no matter what the rest of the world says," said Hopper, putting one hand on his chest. He glared at me again. "Now apologize to Sarah."

"Why?" I said. "I haven't done anything wrong. I'm just stating facts."

"No, you aren't," said Technical. She scowled at me. "You're just trying to force your own reality on the rest of us."

"What?" I said. "I'm not trying to force my—"

"If you don't apologize to Sarah, we'll send you home and never speak to you again," said Incantation.

"That doesn't sound so bad now," I said. I shook my head. "You're all crazy."

"So you want to be put on the NHA's ban list, then," said Incantation.

"Huh?" I said. "What ban list?"

"The NHA maintains a list of neoheroes who are not allowed to join the organization under any circumstances," said Incantation. "And since I am Thaumaturge's apprentice, I have direct access to it. If you refuse to apologize to Sarah, I could have your name on that list and the NHA will never let you join. Ever."

I gulped. "Ever?"

"Ever," Incantation confirmed. She smiled. "You *do* want to join the NHA at some point, yes? Most young neoheroes do. But if you're on that list, not even Omega Man will contest it, because he will know that you are not allowed to be on it."

"This is crazy," I said.

Ghost snorted. "Crazy? Hardly. We're just trying to be inclusive here. You're the crazy one, denying Sarah the right to identify however she wishes. Typical oppressor talk."

I was tempted to just get up and walk away right this instant. I didn't sign up for this. I didn't sign up for any of this. I would rather face my parents' anger at lying to them than apologize to these guys for something I didn't do wrong.

But … I didn't want to be put on the NHA's ban list, either. After all, while my parents might have forbid me from superheroics for the moment, I was going to be an adult and in college next year, which meant I'd have the freedom to what I wanted. And I really wanted to join the NHA, because they were the biggest and best superhero organization in America and in the world. Being put on their ban list would mess up those plans.

Besides, maybe I *was* being too harsh toward Sarah. It seemed ridiculous to me that just 'identifying' as a neohero was enough to be considered one (and it made me wonder whether the rest of the NHA was aware of this), but maybe arguing about it was useless. Would it really hurt me if I just went along with Sarah's, uh, 'identity,' as long as it gave me access to the NHA at some point?

So I made my decision. Although every fiber of my body told me not to, I looked at Sarah and said, "Sarah … I apologize for being mean to you. Can you forgive me?"

Sarah actually looked at me this time. Her tears had vanished, but she still seemed like an emotional time bomb about to go off any moment.

"Why?" said Sarah harshly. "Why should I forgive you for doing the bare minimum? Typical privileged talk. Acting like I *owe* you forgiveness for doing what you're *supposed* to do."

I was about to ask her what the hell she was talking about, but I held my tongue when I saw Incantation shake her head.

So I said, "All right. You are … right. I guess I don't deserve forgiveness for what I did."

"You're damn right," said Sarah. "And I want you to never question my identity ever again. Got it?"

I bit my lower lip, but I nodded slowly and said, "Okay."

Suddenly, Sarah smiled, but it wasn't a kind, friendly smile like we had put all our conflicts behind us. Maybe I was over-thinking things, but she looked just like Robert whenever he successfully bullied someone, like she had just succeeded in dominating me and was pleased with herself for it.

And in a way, I think that she did.

CHAPTER SIX

AFTER THAT, INCANTATION GAVE me a tour of the House, with Ghost tagging along, floating creepily behind us. Sarah, thankfully, did not go with us. She just stayed in the meeting room, where she sat down to watch something on TV. She seemed content now, almost normal; in fact, so normal that I almost wondered if that entire discussion had been a weird hallucination on my part. Both Incantation and Ghost said nothing more about it, further solidifying the strangeness of the situation.

Incantation told me about the House as we walked, but I hardly paid attention. I was so distracted and puzzled about that entire conversation. It felt like I had been hit with an emotional—and mental—pile driver. The shouting and the attacks and the strange emotional outbursts over what seemed to me like minor issues … I just didn't understand it. I had never experienced anything quite like it before. Even Master Chaos hadn't been that crazy.

But I pushed it out of my mind for now. I wanted to focus on the House, so I pulled my mind down to earth and listened to Incantation speaking.

"...So our first stop will be the Training Room," said Incantation. "That's where we train, obviously."

"Huh?" I said, looking at Incantation. "What did you say?"

Incantation looked at me with an irritated expression. "I said, we're going to the Training Room.."

"Oh," I said. "Right. Of course."

Incantation looked at me with annoyance, as if she was wondering why I seemed so out of it. I didn't want to talk to her about Sarah, which I had a feeling would just devolve into another shouting match, so I changed the subject to something else.

"So, uh, your magic," I said as Incantation, Ghost, and I turned a corner, heading toward a large set of doors on the right side of the hall. "How does it work, exactly? I thought neoheroes' powers were … scientific."

I almost said 'biological,' but I worried that Incantation and Ghost might shout at me for daring to push the apparently 'outdated' theory that superpowers had a biological origin. I made a mental note to ask Dad about that later when I went home, because Dad was always on top of the newest developments in science.

"Actually, not all neoheroes receive their powers the same way," said Incantation. She pulled out her wand and twirled it in her hands. "You see, Bolt, my master and I are followers of an ancient magical path that goes back centuries, one known to very few people. It is called the Old Way."

"How did Thaumaturge learn it?" I said. "What is the Old Way, anyway?"

"Like I said, it is an ancient path to learning magic," said

Incantation. "*Real* magic, by the way, not the silly magic tricks you see on TV or on stage. It was founded by an order of ancient magicians in Britain, but went underground after Britain was Christianized. My master learned it from one of its last practitioners, who died ten years ago."

"Can anyone learn the Old Way?" I said. "Or just neoheroes?"

"Pretty much anyone can, but neoheroes have it easier because our bodies are more suited to using it for some reason," said Incantation as the three of them stopped in front of the door to the Training Room. "As far as I know, my master and I are the only two people in the world who practice the Old Way."

"What are the Old Way's limits?" I asked. "Like, can you cast spells Harry Potter style or what?"

Incantation just smiled a mysterious smile at me, which—despite how tense I felt around her and the others—made me wish she hadn't flat out rejected me before. "A magician never reveals her secrets, Bolt."

Before I could ask about that, the Training Room slid open and Incantation and Ghost stepped in, forcing me to follow before the doors closed.

The Training Room was huge. It seemed as wide as a football field, except indoors. The floor, walls, and ceiling were covered in scorch marks, scratches, dents, and other things that showed that the Young Neos must have had some really intense training sessions here. But it was strangely barren, which made me wonder what they were supposed to train against in here.

"This is our Training Room," said Incantation, gesturing at the massive room. "It's open twenty-four hours a day, seven days a week. You can train as much as you like for as long as you like."

"It seems kind of empty, though," I said. "I was expecting some obstacles or training equipment or something."

"Oh, we put it away when we're not training," said Incantation. "You can train against holograms, robots, automated weapons, and pretty much anything else, all controlled by an AI designed by Genius himself."

"An AI?" I said. "What's it called?"

"Reeve," said Incantation. She looked up at the ceiling. "Reeve? Are you there?"

Suddenly, a voice that sounded like an older British gentleman spoke. "Yes, Ms. Incantation, I am here. Would you like to begin your training for the day?"

"No," said Incantation, shaking her head. She gestured at me. "I am just showing Bolt around. He is the son of your creator, Genius."

"He is?" said Reeve. "It is good to meet you, Bolt. Have you joined the Young Neos yet?"

"No," I said, shaking my head. "I'm just here to look around and learn for now."

"Ah," said Reeve. "Of course. Should you need anything, feel free to let me know and I shall do my best to give it to you."

"Thanks, Reeve," said Incantation.

With that, Reeve went silent, but I couldn't help but be reminded of Valerie. I guess Dad must have designed Reeve for the Young Neos or something. It made me wonder just how many AI assistants Dad had made.

Then Incantation looked at me. "Would you like to see the Training Room in action? That's the best way to learn about it."

I nodded. "Sure. I've got the time for—"

THE SUPERHERO'S TEAM

All of a sudden, a loud, screeching noise echoed through the room, making all three of us cringe. At first, I thought that maybe it was some kind of super sonic attack from some villain who had somehow broken into the House, but then I noticed a speaker in the upper right corner of the room from which the noise was blaring.

A voice—Hopper's voice—boomed from the speaker, shouting, "Incantation, Ghost! We've just received a report that the villain Firespirit is attacking a Sagan rally in the Red Town Community Center in Red Town, New York! Thaumaturge has told us to head down there and stop Firespirit ASAP! Come to the Portal Room as fast as you can. We need to leave right away."

The speaker shut off, causing me to look at Incantation and Ghost in confusion. "What? Firespirit? Who's Firespirit?"

"Just another supervillain who we need to be taken down," said Incantation as she and Ghost turned around and started walking out of the Training Room, with me following behind. "We'll have to postpone your tour. Right now, we need to save Sagan before Firespirit kills him."

"We?" I said as I followed Incantation and Ghost down the hall. "Am I coming with you?"

"Do you want to?" said Incantation, glancing over her shoulder at me. "If you want to go home or stay here, that's fine, but we really could use your help."

"Even if I'm not actually a member of the Young Neos?" I said in surprise.

"You don't need to be a Young Neo to help us defeat a villain," Incantation said. "So are you coming or not?"

I considered just going back home, but something in

Incantation's voice made it hard for me to refuse. Besides, I liked fighting and beating supervillains, especially if I saved innocent lives in the process.

So I nodded and said, "Sure, I'll help. I'm always up for a good villain butt-kicking, so just lead the way and I will follow."

The entire team was gathered in the room known as the 'Portal Room,' which was apparently one of the few rooms in the House that was safe for Hopper to use his powers in without risking creating a void that would kill us all. There were no actual Portals here; in fact, it was very empty, but Hopper generated a larger-than-average portal for us that would take us to the Red Town Community Center.

The only Young Neo who stayed back was Sarah, who claimed that she was just too distressed by our earlier conversation in the Meeting Room to go out and fight a supervillain. That seemed ridiculous to me, but I didn't say anything because I knew that if I did, Hopper would probably just open a portal to Antarctica and kick me through it.

Anyway, we ran through the portal and, like before, found ourselves on the other side like we had just walked through a door. We emerged into a large community center, but it was a huge mess. People were running and screaming, chairs and tables were on fire, windows were broken, and more than a few people lay on the floor either dead or injured (it was hard to tell). Barnabas Sagan himself was nowhere to be seen, so I assumed that the Secret Service or his bodyguards had probably already escorted him out.

But that did not mean that Firespirit was no longer a threat. I had never seen Firespirit before, but it was pretty obvious that the mad man standing on the stage laughing like a maniac while throwing fireballs at anything that moved was probably him. He looked like he was in his early thirties and his head was on fire. He wore a yellow jumpsuit that was somehow miraculously not burning to shreds under the intense heat radiating from his body.

"There he is," said Incantation, pointing at Firespirit as the portal behind us closed. She looked at the rest of us. "You guys know what to do, right?"

Ghost, Technical, and Hopper nodded, but I shook my head and said, "No. I'm not familiar with your plans."

"To put it simply, you guys will distract Firespirit while I come up with a spell to take him down," said Incantation. "It's our standard mode of attack."

"Distract? How?" I said.

"However you can," said Incantation. She pointed at Ghost, Technical, and Hopper. "But I want you three to help as many people get out of here as possible. Bolt can distract Firespirit by himself."

The other Young Neos and I nodded. Then we split up, with Ghost, Technical, and Hopper running around trying to help as many people get out of the community center as possible while I ran to meet Firespirit head on.

Firespirit's back was to me because he was lobbing fireballs at the back walls now, which left his back exposed. I grabbed one of the burning chairs as I ran and hurled it at him as hard as I could, watching as it flew through the air toward him.

But then Firespirit suddenly whirled around and unleashed twin fireballs at the chair. The chair exploded, sending burning metal and plastic flying everywhere, while I ducked to avoid getting hit in the face by the debris.

"Who dare throws a chair at the Spirit of Flame?" said Firespirit. He looked down at me. "What is this, a child in spandex? Are you a neohero?"

"Yeah, and I'm also going to stop you," I said. "So unless you want to go to jail with a dent in your head, you should give up while you're ahead."

Firespirit cackled. "How arrogant. Do you not know to whom you are speaking? I am Firespirit, the living embodiment of flame itself! All who stand against me shall be consumed by my hungry flames!"

"No need to ham it up," I said, shaking my head.

"How dare you mock me!" said Firespirit. "Let my flames consume your soul!"

Firespirit lobbed a fireball at me, which I dodged by flying into the air. I tried to get close enough to Firespirit to punch him, but the heat he generated was too intense for me to get close. I just flew around him, trying to distract him as he followed my every movement. He kept lobbing fireballs at me, but I was too fast and he kept missing with every fireball he threw. Still, I hoped Incantation would finish her spell fast, because if she didn't, I had a feeling Firespirit would eventually hit me.

"You've got a bad throwing arm, Firespirit!" I shouted as I avoided another one of his fireballs. "Maybe you should go to the range and get some target practice in!"

Firespirit shouted incoherently. Then his legs exploded into fire and he flew at me, forcing me to swerve out of the way to avoid getting hit. Firespirit blew a hole open in the ceiling and flew through it, causing me to pause in midair and stare in surprise at the flaming hole he had created.

"Bolt! What are you doing?" said Incantation, flying up to me with an annoyed look on his face. Her wand was glowing purple, which I assumed was her spell charging. "You were supposed to distract him while I prepared my spell, not let him get away!"

I shook my head. "Right. I'll see if I can get him back here or at least make sure that he doesn't take his rampage out onto the streets."

I shot through the burning hole before Incantation could say anything else. Flying above the roof of the community center, I stopped in midair and looked around for Firespirit, but he seemed to have disappeared, which was strange because he had only left the community center maybe ten seconds ago. He couldn't be that fast, could he?

Then I heard the crackling of flame above and looked up in time to see Firespirit falling down straight toward me. He collided into me, sending us both crashing down to the roof of the community center. His flames ate at my suit, but it was fireproof, so they did not hurt me.

Still, Firespirit's heat was too intense and uncomfortable. I punched him off me, sending him flying. Firespirit landed on the other side of the roof, rolling briefly before he got back to his feet and summoned two fireballs into his hands as I rose back to my feet. I looked down at my suit, which was smoking slightly, but aside from that my costume seemed to have protected my body from the worst of Firespirit's flames.

"Foolish boy," said Firespirit in a sneering tone. "I admit that you have so far shown yourself to be a formidable opponent, but that does not mean I am going to give up."

"It would be a lot easier for both of us if you did," I said, keeping a careful eye on his burning hands. "Say, why are you attacking this Sagan rally, anyway? If you're angry at him for not following through with his campaign promises when he was elected to the Senate—"

"Politics hardly interests me, boy," said Firespirit. "I was hired to kill Senator Sagan by someone else."

"What?" I said. "Who hired you?"

Firespirit's maniacal grin grew even larger. "Now, now, boy, do you honestly believe that I'll give you that information?"

Firespirit jerked his hands forward and sent a blast of flame at me. I rolled to the side, narrowly avoiding it, and then rolled back to my feet. I tore off a chunk of the roof and threw it at him, but Firespirit blasted it out of the air with a gleeful laugh.

"Is that the best you can do?" said Firespirit. "Throw stuff at me? You are truly pathetic."

"That's not the only trick I have up my sleeve," I said.

I bent over, scooped up a handful of debris, and then started running around Firespirit in a circle using my super speed. As I ran, I pelted Firespirit with the debris, which, coming at such high speed, hit him much harder than normal. Firespirit raised his arms to defend himself, but I still got in a few good hits and even made a cut across his face.

But then Firespirit unleashed a wave of fire from his body, which spread out like a concussive blast. I leaped into the air, narrowly avoiding getting fried, and flew several feet away from him.

Landing on the roof again, I was about to run at him when

Firespirit rocketed through the air toward me with fire shooting from the soles of his boots. He punched me in the face, the fist burning as well as hurting, and I fell to the roof, my eyes watering from the heat.

Before I could get back up, Firespirit slammed his foot down on me, pinning me to the ground. I gasped, because even though my suit was fireproof, the heat from Firespirit's body was incredibly intense at such a close distance.

"Yes, boy, feel the burn," said Firespirit, cackling with glee. He raised his hands, two fireballs appearing in them. "Let your charred corpse be a warning to anyone who dares to stand in the way of Firespirit!"

Just before Firespirit blasted me into oblivion, I heard Incantation shout, "Not so fast!" and, all of a sudden, a blast of water came out of nowhere and struck Firespirit in the side, launching him off me and sending him flying. He crashed into the roof, rolling over and over until he hit the side of the roof, where he lay stunned.

Shaking my head, I looked over and saw Incantation floating toward me. She held her top hat out, which appeared to be where the water blast came from. She put her hat back on just as she landed next to me.

"Bolt, are you okay?" said Incantation, looking down at me, though without any real concern in her eyes.

I groaned, but stood up, wincing at the heat on my chest (though it was rapidly cooling down now that Firespirit wasn't standing on me) and said, "Yeah, I'll be fine. Where were you?"

"Figuring out which spell would work best against Firespirit," said Incantation. "And then getting it ready. I can't use every spell automatically, you know."

"You mean it took you that long to figure out that water puts out fire?" I said in annoyance.

Incantation looked like she was about to respond to that, but then I heard water dripping and looked over at Firespirit.

The assassin was dripping wet. His hair clung to his scalp, while his clothes hung off his rather thin frame. His flames had been completely extinguished, which made him look a lot less threatening than he did before.

"How dare you," said Firespirit, pointing at us dramatically. "You … you put out my flame! No one puts out the Spirit of Flame's fire and gets away with it!"

"You seem surprised that water puts out fire," I said.

"Shut up," said Firespirit. "But this is nothing more than a temporary setback. Die!"

Firespirit jerked his hands out, but no fire came out of his palms. He looked at them in disbelief, which made me wonder if he really *didn't* know that water put out fire.

"No, no, no," said Firespirit. He shook his hands like they were broken. "Come on. Work, damn it. I, the Spirit of Flame, demand that you, my hands, work."

Firespirit's hands must not have thought very highly of him, because they didn't even spark.

Then Firespirit looked up at us, clinching his fists. "Well, I don't need fire to beat up a couple of teenagers anyway!"

Firespirit ran at us, yelling and screaming. Incantation and I exchanged a quick *Is this guy serious?* look before I looked at Firespirit again, who was almost upon us.

With a sigh, I pulled back one fist and punched Firespirit in the face as soon as he was within range of my fist. It wasn't enough to kill him, but it was enough to knock him flat on his back unconscious.

CHAPTER SEVEN

WE TOOK FIRESPIRIT DOWN to the police, who had arrived beforehand but had been unable to enter the building to actually fight Firespirit due to his powers. We also helped the firefighters put out the flames, or really Incantation did, because she was the only one with powers that could actually help. She used her water spell to put out a good chunk of the flame, firing more water from her hat than should have been able to fit in her hat. That made me wonder where the water even came from, but I supposed it was just magic and I wasn't supposed to think about it too deeply.

Standing off to the side with the other Young Neos, I watched as the police, firefighters, and medics helped the survivors get to safety or treated their wounds. Incantation was talking with the police officer who appeared to be in charge of the scene, but she finished speaking with him quickly enough and walked over to us with a satisfied expression on her face.

"Well, it looks like our mission was a success," said Incantation. "According to Officer Jones, only five people of the five hundred in attendance died, although a lot of people are suffering from burns and other wounds. But most of the people are expected to recover, so it all worked out in the end."

"Whew," said Technical, wiping sweat from her brow. "That's good to hear. It was scary in there when Firespirit was throwing fireballs like that. He didn't even seem to have a target. He was just throwing fireballs at anyone or anything in his way."

"Yeah," I said, nodding. "What did the police say they were going to do with him?"

"Officer Jones told me that they were going to transport Firespirit to Ultimate Max, where they will interrogate him to find out why he attacked the Sagan rally," said Incantation.

"I know why he attacked the rally," I said, suddenly remembering what Firespirit had told me during our fight. "He said that he was trying to assassinate Sagan on someone's orders."

"Did he say who hired him?" said Incantation.

I shook my head. "No. He didn't want to tell me. But I wonder who would want to assassinate Senator Sagan."

I looked at the others when I said that, but none of them looked as puzzled as I felt. They looked angry, actually, like they knew who had hired Firespirit to kill Sagan and why.

"I think it's pretty obvious who did it," said Incantation. "Think about it. Who would benefit most from Sagan's death?"

"Um …" I scratched the back of my head as I thought about this. "I'm not sure."

"Plutarch," said Incantation, looking at me in annoyance. "Remember, Sagan is running against Plutarch in the presidential election. If Sagan died, then there would be no one else to run against Plutarch, at least no one else who could beat him."

"Yeah," said Hopper, nodding. "Makes sense. Plutarch is a

monster and a jerk. I could see him doing something like that."

"I don't know," I said. "We don't really have any evidence to prove that Plutarch is behind the assassination attempt, do we? It's possible, obviously, but—"

"It's more than possible," said Technical. She was looking at a screen on her arm, which seemed to show a website. "According to Neo Ranks, Firespirit was one of the Vile Four, along with Steel Skin, Nail Gun, and Plutarch himself."

"So are you saying that Plutarch hired his old friend to kill Sagan?" I said. "How? I thought that the Vile Four were all in prison."

"Not anymore, apparently," said Technical. "According to the news section on New Ranks, The remaining members of the Vile Four were released from Ultimate Max last month, apparently having been bailed out by Plutarch. That's how Firespirit got out."

"Looks like that old bastard is trying to get his old friends to help him," said Incantation, shaking her head. "Plutarch must have offered Firespirit a job because Firespirit was one of his old minions."

"Didn't Plutarch put the Vile Four behind bars himself, though?" I said. "That's why Steel Skin was trying to kill him a week ago. Why would Firespirit accept a job from Plutarch, if that's the case? And why would Plutarch bail him out in the first place?"

"I don't know, maybe he needed the money or something," said Incantation. "All I know is that real villains never change their stripes, especially ones like Plutarch."

I was about to say that I didn't think that that was exactly an airtight case against Plutarch when Ghost suddenly whipped his head to the left and gasped. "Oh my god … it's *him*."

Thinking it was another supervillain or that maybe Firespirit had somehow escaped police custody and was coming after us again, I looked over in the same direction as Ghost, readying my super strength for another fight.

But it turned out that there were only two ordinary people approaching us. One of them was a tall, statuesque thirty-something woman in a black dress, with large gold earrings hanging off her ears. She had a very serious expression on her face and walked like she was a soldier in an army.

Next to the woman was probably the oldest man I had ever seen in my life, who looked so old that I could probably tip him over just by blowing lightly on him. He was very short and stout, with crazy white hair sticking out in all directions. He wore thin glasses on his face that magnified his eyes and also wore a cheap black suit. He walked rather slowly, but based on the way the woman walked next to him, I guessed that he was someone important.

I didn't know who he was, however, so I looked at the others and said, "Who is that guy?"

Ghost looked at me in annoyance. "What? You mean you don't recognize Senator Barnabas Sagan himself?"

I shook my head. "No. I've seen a few pictures of him before, but I'm not that familiar with how he looks."

"Well, that's him," said Ghost. He looked at Sagan again, except this time with a dreamy expression on his face. "He's the man who will save our nation."

I looked at Sagan and thc woman walking by his side as they approached us. Sagan looked nowhere near as imposing or strong as Plutarch, yet I saw a firmness in his eyes that told me that he had the determination to keep fighting no matter what.

Even so, I didn't see any particular reason to treat him special, which made the others' reactions all the stranger. Incantation and Technical were making last minute adjustments to their hair and costumes, while Hopper and Ghost looked like they were ready to fall down on their knees and start worshiping the guy. It was actually kind of creepy, so creepy that I took a small step away from them, just in case they totally lost it.

"Hello there," said Sagan, waving at us with a kindly smile on his face. He had a northeastern accent, maybe from Vermont or something. "You are the Young Neos, correct?"

Incantation looked like she had lost the ability to breathe she was so excited, but she managed a small nod and said, "Yes, sir," in a strangled voice that made me worry for her health.

"Yes, I thought I recognized you," said Sagan, stopping in front of us. He then looked at each one of us in turn. "Incantation, Technical, Ghost, Hopper, and … hmm, I don't recognize you."

Sagan was looking at me when he said that. I noticed that his assistant was also looking at me with a cold stare, like she was daring me to touch Sagan without her permission and give her an excuse to beat me.

Nonetheless, I said in a friendly voice, "I'm Bolt. I'm not actually a member of the Young Neos, at least not yet. I was just helping them beat Firespirit."

"Bolt?" said Sagan. He stroked his chin, like I had just said something very interesting. "You mean the son of Genius? The one who defeated Master Chaos?"

"You know me?" I said in surprise.

"Why, of course," said Sagan. "I'm always keeping up with the next generation of neoheroes, the ones who will defend our country and help us make America a better place for everyone when they grow up."

I glanced at Incantation, who looked like she was about to die of happiness. So did the others, for that matter, including Ghost, who was probably going to become an actual ghost if his happiness at Sagan's praise was as real as it seemed.

"I just wanted to thank you all for quickly defeating Firespirit and keeping the deaths of my supporters to a minimum," said Sagan. He shuddered. "If you had not arrived in time, why, I am certain that today would have become one of the bloodiest days in American history."

"I-It was nothing, Senator Sagan," said Incantation with a stutter. "We do this sort of thing every day."

"I know, but I must still thank you all anyway," said Sagan. "I cannot give you any gifts, but you have convinced me that the safety of our country is in good hands if you five represent the next generation of neoheroes."

Sagan sounded like he really meant that. He looked at each one of us in the eyes when he spoke and I saw nothing but sincerity in his own eyes. I was starting to understand why the Young Neos liked him.

"You're welcome, Senator," I said. "By the way, are you a neohero yourself?"

Sagan chuckled a grandfatherly chuckle. "Oh, no, I have no powers of my own, though I have family that does. And my assistant, June, here happens to be a telepath."

Sagan gestured at the tall woman standing next to him, the

one I had noticed before. She didn't say anything. She just nodded at us, which made her seem uptight to me, but I said nothing about it.

"Why do you have a telepath as your assistant?" I asked.

"Because June is a hard-working and loyal woman who has been by my side from the very beginning of my campaign when I started last year," Sagan replied. "Her telepathy also helps keep me safe. More than once, June has detected the thoughts of a nearby assassin planning to kill or harm me to take me out of the race. I owe her my life many times over."

June didn't even look embarrassed by Sagan's praise. She just looked smug and satisfied, like she was aware of how awesome she was and was glad that Sagan was telling us about it.

"But even though I am not a neohero myself, I will still fight for neohero rights," said Sagan, putting a hand on his chest. "Unlike some people, I trust you neoheroes and see you as allies, rather than enemies, of the United States. Certainly there are bad people among you, like that awful Firespirit, but by and large you are our friends and I will make sure to fight for your rights no matter what."

It seemed to me like Sagan was really trying to sell himself to us. Then again, he was running for President and he needed every vote he could get, although it was strange because none of us were of voting age yet.

"Thanks, Senator," said Incantation. "We know your record and your unwavering support of our community. None of us can vote yet, but we believe in you and your vision and think you will make a great President."

"Thank you for the support, young lady," said Sagan. "Now

June and I must be leaving. We have to return to my hotel so I can get some rest before I speak with the press later today about this attack. Firespirit's attack took a lot out of me."

"Of course," said Incantation. "We completely understand. Next time you need our help, don't be afraid to call us."

"I won't," said Sagan.

With that, Sagan and June turned around and walked away. But before they got very far, I remembered something urgent and said, "Senator, wait. I have something important to tell you."

Sagan and June stopped and looked over their shoulders at me in surprise.

"Yes?" said Sagan, who sounded a little annoyed at being stopped. "What is it?"

"Firespirit told me that he was hired by someone to kill you," I said. "He didn't say who, but this was definitely an assassination attempt on your life."

Sagan paused. For a moment, he looked almost worried, but then he shook his head and said, "Thank you for letting me know, young man. I will be sure to share that information with the police later, when I speak with them about this terrible tragedy."

Then Sagan and June resumed walking away until they reached a limo which seemed to have been rented for Sagan. Sagan entered the limo, as did June, and then it drove away down the street into town until it turned a corner and was out of sight.

Once they were gone, I suddenly felt a pressure on my mind lift, a mental pressure I hadn't even noticed until Sagan and June had left. It was like someone had just lifted a huge boulder off my back and it actually madc me feel a little dizzy, even nauseated, though I wasn't sure where it came from.

But before I could bring this up to the others, Technical squealed. “Oh my god! We got to meet *Sagan* himself. In person!”

“And he knew our names, too,” said Hopper with a sigh. “I always knew he was an awesome guy, but I didn't know he was *that* awesome.”

“Meeting him was almost like a religious experience,” said Ghost. He looked up at the sky wistfully. “How can such pure people live on this sinful earth?”

“I know,” said Incantation. “He's utterly amazing.”

I frowned. “He seems like a nice guy, but I don't see what's so great about him. He didn't seem all that special to me.”

“Not special?” said Ghost, looking at me like I had just suggested that we torture a puppy. “But didn't you *feel* the kindness that radiated from him? He's … oh god, I can't even describe him right now. He's amazing.”

“Well, I didn't see anything that interesting about him,” I said. “But whatever. What's important is that we saved a lot of innocent lives and stopped a supervillain. Now what?”

“Now we go back to the House,” said Incantation. She looked at Hopper. “Hopper, open a portal back. I need to report back to Thaumaturge with the results of our successful mission.”

“Sure thing,” said Hopper.

He raised a hand and a portal opened nearby. Because I was the nearest, I walked through it first, feeling tired but happy about how the mission went. If this was how most Young Neo missions went, well, then maybe I would join the team after all.

At least, that was what I thought until I walked straight into Dad.

THE SUPERHERO'S TEAM

CHAPTER EIGHT

DAD STOOD IN THE Portal Room, standing right in front of me with his arms folded over his chest. He was in his full Genius costume, his face hidden behind the visor of his helmet, but his body language left no room for any confusion about how he felt.

"Oh," I said, staring up at Dad in surprise. "Dad, uh, what are you doing here?"

Dad didn't answer. He just looked down at me, making me feel very small, even though he wasn't that much taller than me.

Then I heard a gasp behind me and I looked over my shoulder. Incantation, Technical, Ghost, and Hopper had stepped through the portal, which was closed now, and were staring at Dad with even more surprise than me. Technical even looked like she was about to faint.

"Huh?" said Hopper, rubbing his eyes and then lowering his hands to look at Dad more closely. "No way … are you Genius?"

"Yes," said Dad. His tone was curt. "You are the Young Neos, correct?"

"Yeah," said Hopper. "That's us."

Dad nodded and then looked at Incantation. "And you are Thaumaturge's apprentice, yes?"

Incantation nodded. "Yes. Why do you ask?"

"Because I am wondering if your master is aware that my son is here when he isn't supposed to be," said Dad. His tone was flat now, but I could still sense the disappointment within it. "If I recall correctly, the correct protocol is that you have to first receive approval from Thaumaturge before inviting someone into the House or anywhere else on Hero Island."

Incantation's face suddenly went pale. "Um, Genius, you know, it really was—"

"And I should probably report this to your master," said Dad, interrupting Incantation like she wasn't even speaking. "I wonder how he would react if he learned that you invited someone into the House without his knowledge. I haven't spoken with Thaumaturge in years, but I remember that he never liked it whenever anyone bypassed his authority for any reason, even if that person was his family."

"Please don't tell him," said Incantation, putting her hands together and looking at Dad with fear. "We didn't mean anything bad by it. We planned to tell him and—"

"Don't worry," Dad interrupted her again. "I won't tell him because you have not, as far as I know, done anything wrong or hurt anyone. He would probably never listen to me anyway, even if I dragged Bolt to him."

Incantation sighed in relief. "Oh, thank you."

Dad suddenly put his hand on my shoulder, but still did not look at me. "Instead, I am going to take Bolt home. We're going to have a little talk about telling the truth."

I tried not to show any fear, but it was hard because I knew that Dad was not going to show me any mercy. I looked over my shoulder at the others, but none of them looked like they were going to come to my rescue.

But then, all of a sudden, Technical stepped forward. She looked really shy and timid, not even meeting Dad's gaze, but she said, “Um, Mr. Genius, sir?”

“Yes?” said Dad. “What is it? Do you have something important to tell me?”

“I just wanted to ask …” Technical took a deep breath, like she was about to ask for something very serious. She held out her mechanical arm and said, “Can I have your autograph? On my arm? Please?”

Although Dad's face was not visible, I could tell that Technical's request had taken him by surprise. “What?”

“It's just, um, I'm a really big fan and I really admire your work and I just can't believe I'm meeting you and I know your son,” said Technical, who was talking so fast I couldn't keep up with her even if I used my super speed. “So, uh, I just want your autograph, please?”

“Sorry, but I do not give out autographs, even to fans,” said Dad. “But I am glad you appreciate my work. Did you make that mechanical arm yourself?”

Technical nodded. “Yes. I based it off your artificial limb blueprints, the ones you never actually made.”

“You mean the Synth Limbs?” said Dad in surprise. “I didn't know anyone else was interested in them.”

“Well, I was and I figured out how to do it, so I made this arm for myself when I lost my old one,” said Technical. “I followed your blueprints exactly and it works perfectly, though I made a few minor modifications."

"Interesting," said Dad. "While I'd love to examine your arm to see how my ideas actually work in real life, I'm afraid Bolt and I must be leaving. But you should send me pictures of your arm so I can examine them later, okay?"

Technical looked like she could hardly believe her luck. She just managed to squeak out, "Yes, sir," before looking away like she was overcome with embarrassment.

"All right," said Dad. "But before we leave, I want to let you know that this is the only time I will not tell Thaumaturge about this. If I catch you do anything like this again, I will not hesitate to tell Thaumaturge, both about that and this one, too."

"Don't worry, Genius, sir," said Incantation quickly. "We promise never to invite your son here ever again without your knowledge."

"Yeah," said Hopper. "It wasn't really our fault, anyway. Bolt insisted that we invite him."

I glared at Hopper. "Whose side are you on?"

Hopper just shrugged, while Dad said, "Well, I hope you behave better in the future. Come on, Bolt. Let's leave."

Before I could say good bye to the Young Neos, Dad turned the Teleportation Buckle on his belt and suddenly we were standing in the living room of our house again. I blinked several times before looking at Dad, who removed his helmet.

"Honey," Dad called, "I got Kevin back."

A second later, Mom stepped out of the kitchen. She looked incredibly worried and angry; not quite as worried as she looked back when Master Chaos was around, but still worried anyway.

"Hi, Mom," I said, giving her my best smile while waving at her slightly. "I—"

"Why did you lie to us?" said Mom, interrupting me before I could even think of what I wanted to say. She may not have been a neohero herself, but her angry and worried tone made me cringe nonetheless.

"Lie to you?" I said. "I wouldn't exactly call it *lying*—"

"Yes, it is," said Dad, causing me to look at his disapproving face. "You told us you were going to spend the weekend at Malcolm's place. But you lied."

"Well, okay, I lied," I said, throwing my hands up into the air. "I mean, how did you even find out?"

"Valerie told me," said Dad.

My earcom crackled to life and Valerie said, "I am so sorry, Bolt, but I just couldn't keep your real location a secret to Genius forever. My programming makes it impossible for me to lie, so I had to tell him where you really went."

"It's all right, Val, I understand," I said. "You don't need to say anything. This conversation doesn't have much to do with you."

"Okay," said Valerie, though she still sounded apologetic.

Then my earcom crackled off, and as soon as it did, Mom said, "Kevin, why did you lie to us?"

Both Mom and Dad were looking at me with the hardest glares in the world. I felt like I was being interrogated, but I tried to keep my cool anyway, because I didn't want to behave like I was guilty of anything.

"Well, I just wanted to see what the Young Neos were like," I said. "I wasn't going to *stay* in the House with them. I was just trying to see if I'd be a good fit for the team."

"Even when we told you that you couldn't join?" said Dad. He sighed in frustration. "Kevin, were you even listening to what I told you a week ago?"

"I was," I said defensively. "I just didn't see any harm in going there and seeing what their base was like. I was planning to come home on Sunday."

"It doesn't matter what you were planning to do," said Dad, shaking his head. "You lied to us and went somewhere you are not supposed to without our permission. You even got Valerie in on the lie."

"I know, I know," I said, holding up my hands. "But I don't see the problem. No one was hurt; well, except for Firespirit, I guess, and the people he killed at the Sagan rally."

"You fought a supervillain at a Sagan rally?" said Mom, sounding even more stricken than Dad. "A supervillain who *killed* innocent people?" Her eyes darted to my chest, which was still smoking slightly from where Firespirit had hit it. "Is that smoke?"

"He was trying to kill Sagan," I said. "And we managed to stop him without any of us getting killed. It's not a big deal."

"Risking your life to fight a supervillain assassin isn't a big deal?" said Mom. She looked like she was about to faint. "Kevin, I know you have super strength and all, but that was still dangerous."

"I know, but so what?" I said. I patted my chest. "I'm still alive and breathing and Firespirit is going straight to Ultimate Max. He's not going to hurt anyone else for a long time."

"That doesn't change the fact that this is your second

supervillain fight in a week," said Dad, "even though we told you that we didn't want you fighting supervillains unless they attack you first."

"Well, maybe I *like* the superhero life, have you ever thought of that?" I said in annoyance. "You know I don't go hunting down supervillains, but if there's a crazy guy throwing fireballs at innocent people or a big shirtless guy trying to smash someone into paste, well, it's my duty to stop them because of my power. I thought you'd understand that, Dad."

"I do understand it," said Dad. "But I do not agree with it. Nor do I agree with your interest in the Young Neos."

"Why not?" I said. "Sure, they're a little weird, but I'd still like to be on the team. They could provide me with all sorts of ways to develop my powers. Why are you against me joining them?"

Mom and Dad exchanged looks, like they were trying to decide what to tell me. I didn't really know what they were so worried about me knowing. I just folded my arms over my chest and waited for their response.

Then Dad looked at me and said, "We just don't want you putting your life in danger like that. We just want you to live a normal life."

I could tell they had other reasons for not wanting me to join the Young Neos, but I was in no mood to find out their real reasons.

I just said, "Well, I'm almost an adult, Dad. Soon, I'll be out of the house and able to do what I want with my life. You won't be able to tell me what groups I can and can't join, so maybe you should just accept that I'm going to do what I want."

"You're right that soon you'll be an adult and out of the

house," said Dad. "I also cannot really stop you from doing superheroics."

"See? We agree," I said. "So—"

"So I'll just take your super suit from you until you graduate," said Dad.

"Wait, what?" I said. I put my hands on my body, which was still covered by my suit. "You can't take my suit away from me."

"Yes, I can," said Dad. He held out his hand. "After all, I gave it to you in the first place, and because you are still under my authority, that means I have some control over what you wear. Besides, you can't fight crime or supervillains without your suit, seeing as you have been working very hard to keep your identity a secret from the world."

My hands balled into fists and I looked at Mom in desperation. "Mom, you don't agree with Dad, do you?"

"Actually, I do," said Mom. "If that is what will keep you from putting yourself into needlessly dangerous situations, then I am in full support of your father's decision to confiscate your costume."

I considered just running out of the house and leaving Mom and Dad behind, but then I realized that Dad would probably just catch me somehow anyway. Besides, I bet the suit-up watch was connected to Dad's other devices, meaning that he could probably take it from me regardless of what I did.

So, reluctantly, I pressed the button on my suit-up watch and, in an instant, I was back in my street clothes. Then I removed the watch from my wrist and handed it to Dad, who took it without a word and put it into one of the pockets of his own super suit.

"When will I get it back?" I asked.

"After you graduate, of course," said Dad, looking at me again.

My eyes widened. "After I graduate? That's a year away."

"I know," said Dad. "I don't want you doing any sort of superheroics while you are in school. With Master Chaos gone, there's really no good reason for you to use your powers or fight crime. You can pass your tests without needing to fly."

I looked at Mom again, but as always, she seemed to support Dad's decision wholeheartedly.

So my shoulders slumped. "Then I guess I'm going back to school on Monday, then."

"Yes," said Dad. "I am sorry, Kevin, but we just want what is best for you. That's all."

I nodded, but deep down, I was angry and annoyed. "Okay. I'll just go back to my bedroom, then."

With that, I turned and left the living room, making my way to my bedroom, but slowly. I was now wondering if my superhero career was over, because despite what Dad said, I had a feeling I would never be getting my suit back. This was going to be a *long* year, that was for sure.

CHAPTER NINE

INSTEAD OF SPENDING THE weekend cooped up in my room, I actually called Malcolm and asked him to meet me for lunch at Rod's Burgers, a local burger joint in town. I needed to talk with him about what happened, so he agreed to meet me there tomorrow.

So on Sunday, at lunch, I went to Rod's Burgers, ordered one of Rod's famous burgers from the cashier, and then went and sat down at one of the few unoccupied booths in the place, my mouth watering at the delicious smell of the burger. The restaurant was packed, mostly from the church crowd, many of whom were just getting out of church. Thus, everyone was dressed really nicely, except for me, which would have made me feel awkward under normal circumstances but I was too distracted by the idea that I would never be a superhero again to care about that. I just kept an eye out for Malcolm, who had texted me that he would be there soon.

Malcolm arrived roughly ten minutes after me. Like most of the other restaurant goers, he was dressed in nicer-than-usual clothes, a red button down shirt and tan slacks, though I noticed that his necklace was still tucked into his shirt. He got his order and then came over to my booth, where he sat down opposite me with his burger and drink.

"Were you at church or something?" I said to Malcolm, looking at his nice clothes in surprise.

Malcolm shrugged, though he seemed more embarrassed than nonchalant. "Yeah. My family is big into church. We were going to go to lunch together but I told 'em I was going to eat lunch with you. Didn't have time to change."

"Huh," I said. "I didn't know you were a Christian."

"Yeah, I am, but it's not that important," said Malcolm. He leaned toward me, his eyes wide with excitement. "I saw on the news that you and the Young Neos saved Sagan from that crazy fire guy."

I looked around us briefly, but none of the other customers was paying attention to us. Everyone was too busy eating and talking to each other to listen to our conversation, but I was still careful to keep my voice low just to minimize the chances of someone hearing us.

"Was that on the news?" I said in surprise, looking at Malcolm again. "I haven't been paying attention."

"Yeah," said Malcolm, nodding eagerly. He sipped from his drink. "It was really awesome. It didn't affect your Neo Rank, but it was mentioned on the Sagan for President Facebook page."

"Huh," I said. "Did the news report mention anything in particular?"

"Nah," said Malcolm, shaking his head. "Just said you and the Young Neos defeated Firespirit. Sagan gave a really inspiring speech afterward, talking about how he was still a firm supporter of neohero rights and stuff even after this and how he was going to keep going no matter what. It was awesome."

I took a bite out of my burger. "That's what he told us, more or less, after we stopped Firespirit."

"Wait, you mean *you* got to actually *talk* with Sagan?" said Malcolm, his jaw dropping. "Like, face to face?"

"Yep," I said. "He seemed nice."

"Nice? That man's amazing," said Malcolm with a sigh. "Way better than Plutarch in every possible way." He scowled. "I didn't even pay attention to what Plutarch said about it. Something about it being proof that superhumans are dangerous or something. I dunno. He's an idiot."

I didn't really care about Sagan or Plutarch, so I said, "The Young Neos also seemed to like Sagan a lot."

Malcolm suddenly frowned. "Hey, why are you talking about the Young Neos like you're not one of them?" Then he glanced at my wrist. "Where'd your suit-up watch go?"

Sensing a good moment, I explained to Malcolm what happened yesterday, keeping it as brief as I could. I omitted the bit about Sarah Jane Watson, however, because I wasn't sure what to make of that craziness. I just told him about how I went to the House, my meeting with the Young Neos, and how we defeated Firespirit. I also explained about how Mom and Dad took my suit-up watch away.

"Damn," said Malcolm, leaning back in his seat after I finished. "So you're not a member of the Young Neos *and* you can't be a superhero anymore?"

I nodded glumly. "Sadly. It means I'm just going to have to be a normal high schooler for now."

"Aw, man," said Malcolm. "This is really unfair. You should complain to the NHA or something."

"What good would that do?" I said as I sipped from my drink. "Dad isn't even a member of the NHA anymore."

"Good point," said Malcolm. "Still, I wish there was some way I could help. After saving Sagan, I think you deserve a hero's reward or something. But your parents are treating you like you're a kid."

"I know," I said. "But what can I do? I'm still just a teen. Until I move out of my parents' house—which probably won't be until next year—I'm pretty powerless."

Malcolm rubbed his forehead, a frown crossing his face. "Geez, man, I don't know. I wish I had superpowers of my own that I could use to help you."

"Thanks for the thought, but it's okay," I said with a sigh. "The world already has plenty of superheroes, after all, so it's not like I'm really needed."

"But the world can always use more heroes," said Malcolm. "At least, I'd feel safer knowing you could use your powers here in Silvers if nothing else, even though Silvers is a pretty safe town aside from the occasional drunk driver."

I shrugged and took another bite out of my burger. "I agree, but there's not much I can do—"

A hand fell on my shoulder, causing me to look up, burger still in my mouth, and see a tall Asian man in an overcoat standing behind me. It was Triplet, who was getting strange, furtive glances from the other customers, glances he seemed to ignore entirely. He was looking down at me with a comically serious expression.

"Kevin Jason?" said Triplet.

I nodded. "Um, Tr—"

"Shh," said Triplet, holding up one finger to his lips. He glanced around before looking at me again. "Don't say my name in public."

I could feel the other people looking at me, but I tried to keep my focus on Triplet, hoping that maybe the other customers would lose interest if I didn't look at them. "Um, okay."

"I need to speak with you," said Triplet. He gestured with his head at the entrance. "Outside."

I put my burger down, not sure if I should accept or reject his request. I glanced at Malcolm, who seemed just as confused about Triplet's appearance as the other customers were.

"What do you want to talk about?" I said, looking at Triplet again.

"Something important," said Triplet. "Can't be more specific than that."

I frowned, but then I remembered that Triplet was one of Dad's friends, so I doubted Triplet was up to anything nefarious.

So I nodded and said, "Sure. Will it be for long?"

"Probably not," said Triplet. "Just need to ask you a few questions."

I wondered what these questions were, but I didn't ask any questions of my own. I just told Malcolm I'd be back in a bit and followed Triplet out the front entrance. We walked over to the back of the restaurant, hidden from view of the parking lot and the road.

But we were not alone. Triplet was already leaning against the back of the restaurant, his arms folded over his chest. He looked over at us as the Third (which was what I realized this Triplet had to be) and I made our way over to him.

"Ah, there you are," said Triplet, pushing himself off the back of the building and shoving his hands into the pockets of his overcoat. "Good job, Third."

The Third didn't say anything. It just walked back into Triplet, causing him to glow blue briefly before his body returned to normal. Triplet patted his chest for a moment before looking at me. "Hello, Kevin. Do you remember me?"

I nodded. "Yes. But did you have to send one of your Thirds to get me?"

"I couldn't risk being caught in there," said Triplet. He looked around again, like he thought someone might be listening to us nearby, even though we were alone. "My investigation has uncovered some dangerous facts that could put my life at risk if they become common knowledge. Just being out here in the open is dangerous."

"Why?" I said. I glanced back the way I came. "And what does this have to do with me? I have a burger back in there that I need to finish and I hate letting my food go cold."

"Because you know some stuff that I don't," said Triplet. "I saw the news reports on your battle with Firespirit at the Sagan rally."

I looked at Triplet again. "So? What does that have to do with anything?"

"I have some questions to ask you about it," said Triplet. "It is related to my investigation."

"The investigation you can't tell me anything about, right?" I said. "Because you keep your clients' problems confidential?"

"Normally, I don't share my clients' problems with other people, but I trust you enough to let you know what I am investigating," said Triplet. He looked me in the eye. "But you have to promise me not to share this information with anyone else. Not even with your own father."

Not even with Dad? That piqued my interest. "Sure. My lips are sealed."

"Good," said Triplet. "Honest and trustworthy, just like your father. Anyway, I have been hired to investigate Adam Lucius Plutarch. Do you know who he is?"

"Of course," I said. "I met him once. But why are you investigating him? And who hired you?"

"I don't know the identity of my client," Triplet admitted. "He came to me through an intermediary, asking me to investigate Plutarch's background. My client calls himself the Citizen, though I don't know anything else about him beyond that."

"Is that normal?" I said. "I mean, not knowing your client's identity?"

"No, but I was told that the Citizen was afraid of suffering retaliation if someone found out that he was hiring me to investigate Plutarch, so I didn't ask about it," said Triplet. "Besides, he pays well, and as long as I get paid, I can put up with a lot of eccentricities I might normally not tolerate."

I snorted. Eccentricities? That was rich coming from a guy who didn't trust hotels.

Nonetheless, I said, "But why Plutarch? Is he up to anything bad?"

"Possibly," said Triplet. He looked around again, which seemed to be a habit of his. "Plutarch used to be known as the

Billionaire. He gave the NHA a lot of trouble before retiring from crime in 2005 and helping the G-Men arrest many of his former allies and minions. He has not, to my knowledge, been involved in any criminal activities since then."

"So why are you investigating him if he's reformed?" I said.

"Because the Citizen believes that Plutarch is planning to turn America into a dictatorship," said Triplet. "He is worried that Plutarch has merely been biding his time since his 'retirement' and is taking advantage of America's disgust with the political establishment to be elected to the presidency and make himself into a dictator."

"Really?" I said. I gulped. "Do you have any evidence to support that?"

"I've uncovered some troubling facts," said Triplet. "For example, I discovered that Plutarch apparently made a visit to Ultimate Max in 2010 to speak with the jailed members of the Vile Four. I've also learned that Plutarch paid for their bail and that Steel Skin, Firespirit, and Nail Gun's whereabouts were unknown until their recent attacks at the Plutarch and Sagan rallies."

"Are you saying that Plutarch hired his old supervillain friends to help him takeover America?" I said.

"It is possible, but I am still investigating," said Triplet. "That is certainly one conclusion that the facts seem to be pointing toward at the moment. And that is also why I am in Texas; I heard from my sources that Steel Skin was planning to attack the Plutarch rally and I came down here to speak with him."

"But Steel Skin tried to *kill* Plutarch," I pointed out. "He really seemed to hate the guy. Why would he help Plutarch win the election if he hates him?"

"True, but I think it is possible that it was all an act," said Triplet. "Remember, Plutarch runs on an anti-neohero campaign. What better way to prove his point about the dangerousness of superhumans than by having one attack one of his rallies on live TV?"

"What about Firespirit, then?" I said. "He attacked the Sagan rally."

"I believe he was also hired by Plutarch to do that," said Triplet. "But that's why I am talking with you. I've heard rumors that Firespirit was a hired assassin. Is that true?"

I nodded. "Firespirit told me he was hired by someone to kill Sagan. He didn't say who, though."

"I knew it," said Triplet. "Prior to joining the Vile Four, Firespirit was a well-known assassin. It's no surprise that he's up to his old tricks and likely still working for Plutarch. I bet Plutarch hired Firespirit to kill Sagan."

"That's what the other Young Neos thought," I said. "But we don't have any way to prove that. I know that the police were going to interrogate him, but—"

"They have," Triplet interrupted me. "And they found out that Firespirit's memory has been wiped."

"Wiped?" I said. "What? When did this happen?"

"Sometime last night," said Triplet. He pulled out of his smartphone and started tapping the screen. "There was an article on Neo Ranks that said that Franklin Burns, which is Firespirit's real name, claimed that he could not remember the identity of the person who had hired him to kill Sagan."

"What?" I said. "Is he lying?"

"It doesn't look like it," said Triplet. He looked up at me again. "I suspect that Steel Skin has suffered a similar fate, because recent news reports have stated that Steel Skin doesn't know why he is in Ultimate Max or how he got there."

"They can't both be suffering from amnesia, can they?" I said.

"Of course not," said Triplet. "Their memory was obviously wiped by someone who didn't want the police knowing who they are working for." He looked at his phone again. "Here's the article. See?"

Triplet showed me his phone, which displayed an article on Neo Ranks with the headline 'FRANKLIN 'FIRESPIRIT' BURNS CLAIMS TO HAVE FORGOTTEN IDENTITY OF CLIENT WHO HIRED HIM TO KILL SAGAN.' It showed a picture of a confused-looking Firespirit sitting in the back of a police cruiser with his hands cuffed.

Pulling back, I said, "What's going on, then? Who is doing this?"

"Someone in Plutarch's employ, most likely," said Triplet as he put his phone back into the pocket of his overcoat. "Likely a superhuman with mind powers. I used to know a guy who could alter and rearrange memories and even delete them outright. Such a person would be useful for any politician seeking to craft a narrative that will help him get elected."

"Does Plutarch have any known superhumans in his campaign?" I said.

"Just a few, but none of them have any mind powers," said Triplet. "But telepaths are a tricky bunch. They are extremely good at hiding their real identities and powers from everyone. For example, back in the late nineties I visited a small town in upstate

New York that was ruled by a telepath who used his mind powers to alter the memories and perceptions of the town's inhabitants so he could rule without anyone even suspecting that he was there. He was touch to catch."

I shuddered. "That's a scary thought."

"But most telepaths are nowhere near that powerful or malicious," said Triplet. "All you need is just one telepath who is really good at erasing or altering memories and no one could ever link you to any crime you don't want them linking you to."

"Is there any way I can help in your investigation?" I asked.

"No," said Triplet. "You've already helped me a great deal by confirming that Firespirit is indeed an assassin. I suspect Plutarch hired him in order to make Sagan supporters more anti-neohero and thus likely to vote for him, considering how Sagan has tried to show himself as the pro-neohero candidate in this election."

"Well, I hope you figure out what Plutarch is doing," I said. "It sounds dangerous."

"That it is," said Triplet. "Anyway, I'm leaving now."

"To where?" I said. "Back to New York?"

"Can't tell you," said Triplet. "It's a secret."

I rolled my eyes. "Is everything a secret with you?"

"Everything worth knowing is," Triplet said. "Anyway, good bye. I hope you get your super suit back at some point."

With that, Triplet turned and walked away down the street, leaving me feeling more confused—and worried—than ever.

CHAPTER TEN

IT WAS HARD TO go back to school on Monday after my conversation with Triplet. While I knew that the investigation had nothing to do with me, I was still thinking about it. After all, if what Triplet said was true, then Plutarch needed to be stopped. Here we had an actual supervillain running for President and, according to some of the online polls I looked up, he had a very good chance of winning the entire election.

But what was I supposed to do? Without my super suit, I could hardly fly to Plutarch's campaign headquarters and confront the man there myself. Dad still had my super suit locked away somewhere, which meant that I couldn't do any sort of superheroics on my own. I was forced to go to school, go home, and do my homework every day. It didn't help that I couldn't talk about it with anyone because I had promised to Triplet that I would not tell anyone the details of his investigation. I didn't even tell Malcolm when I went back into the restaurant; I just told him that Triplet had some questions to ask me and that I had promised not to tell anyone about it. Malcolm seemed to understand, but he also seemed frustrated, which I understood.

It didn't help, of course, that the whole 'Plutarch VS Sagan' debate seemed to follow me wherever I went. Malcolm and Tara were still not talking to each other due to the polarization, and whenever they did talk to each other, it was just more pointless political debate that got nowhere fast. I found myself siding with Malcolm more often than not, now that I knew about Triplet's investigation, but I still got annoyed by the debate. It was easier to do, however, knowing that Robert was a big Plutarch supporter and wore Plutarch's MANA hat almost everywhere he went unless a teacher asked him to remove it.

Nor did I talk with my parents about it, either. I was sure that Dad already knew about Triplet's investigation, because that was what I suspected they had been talking about when Triplet came to our house that one time, but I was still too angry with my parents about their taking my super suit away to speak to them much. That didn't seem to bother my parents, probably because they thought I would be over it soon.

When I got home from school on Monday, I just went straight to my room, not even bothering to ask Mom when dinner would be ready. Closing the door to my room, I dropped my backpack on the floor, walked over to my bed, and lay down on it. Maybe I'd take a quick nap, just to forget my troubles for a while, but I doubted I'd wake up any happier.

I wish there was some way I could investigate Plutarch myself; some way I could meet him, maybe get close to his headquarters and see if I could find any clues to find out what he was up to. Yeah, I knew the case really had nothing to do with me, but if there was a way I could help find out thc truth, then I would.

Some way to meet him …

Suddenly, I sat up from my bed and dashed over to my backpack. Undoing the flap, I dug through my backpack's various pockets and pouches until I felt some paper, which I fished out of the pack and held up to the light to see better.

It was the card that Plutarch had given me a week ago, when I saved him from Steel Skin. It had all of his contact information on it, which meant that I had direct access to him. I grabbed my phone and was about to put in the number on the card when I caught myself.

Why would Plutarch ever want to meet me? He knew me as Bolt, sure, but he didn't know who Kevin Jason was and I certainly didn't want him knowing my real identity, especially if he was as bad as Triplet believed he was. I needed some way to arrange a meeting with Plutarch but without him knowing who I was.

But Dad still had my suit and I doubted he'd let me have it back long enough to have a meeting with Plutarch, who I knew Dad hated just as much as anybody. I'd have a tough time convincing him to give me my suit back, especially after he told me he was not going to give it back to me until after graduation.

But maybe I didn't need my suit. Maybe I could make my own.

I looked at my closet and at a few boxes of my clothes that were still unpacked from the move. An idea was starting to form, an idea I wasn't sure would work, but I had no choice but to put it into action if I was going to meet Plutarch.

Getting up from my bed, I walked over to my closet, opened the door, and started looking for whatever I could find, anything that would help me make my new costume.

Yeah, I knew it looked silly. Yeah, I knew it probably wouldn't hold up well in a fight, if at all. Yeah, I knew it probably looked stupid.

But I was desperate. I needed a costume and I didn't have access to my better one. I couldn't just go flying around in my street clothes, not unless I wanted people to know my secret identity, anyway.

That was why I felt awkward as I flew through the air toward the Texas office of the Plutarch campaign, which was located outside of Fallsville. My suit was simple: A large, black hoodie, with the hood pulled firmly over my face, and an old blue ski mask from last winter. I wore a pair of faded jeans, plus some old tennis shoes I thought I had gotten rid of but apparently had simply stashed in the further reaches of my closet and forgotten about. I had also found some old, cracked goggles and some fingerless gloves that I wore just to make myself even less recognizable to anyone who might see me.

I must have looked strange to anyone below … well, if anyone could actually *see* me, anyway. I was flying fast and high, too high for most people to see me. It helped that it was cloudy today, but I kept thinking that the clouds were going to explode and start pouring rain on me, which would suck.

But at least Plutarch had agreed to meet with me. Back on Monday, I called up his office and asked if I could meet with Plutarch sometime. His assistant—who had answered the phone—agreed and we got an in-person meeting scheduled for Friday evening. I was actually surprised at how easily I got the meeting scheduled, but Plutarch's assistant told me that he was a big fan of mine and had given her orders to put me in his schedule if I called. That seemed suspicious to me, but I was never one to question good luck whenever it came my way.

Obviously, I had not told my parents about this. Perhaps it technically wasn't superheroics, but it came too close for my liking. I very much doubted that my parents would approve of me going to meet Plutarch, especially Dad, who didn't like Plutarch at all. I didn't think I'd be in any trouble, given that Plutarch wasn't a superhuman and didn't seem likely to harm me, but I would never be able to convince my parents of that, so I had to leave without them knowing.

Instead, I told them that I was going to hang out with Malcolm and Tara tonight, which they accepted. Even Dad didn't seem suspicious about it, probably because I didn't have my super suit. He probably thought that I wouldn't sneak out of town to meet with an ex-supervillain presidential candidate without my suit. Well, I guess Dad didn't expect me to be so creative. And there was no way for Dad to track me, either, because I didn't bring my earcom with me, mostly because I knew that I couldn't trust Valerie to keep secrets for me anymore.

Soon, I saw the campaign headquarters for the Plutarch campaign in Texas, which was a large mansion that looked really expensive. It was located outside of Fallsville, with tall fenced gates and a beautiful green lawn and even a large pond to go with it. I was told that the campaign headquarters was in one of Plutarch's mansions because Plutarch preferred having his campaign staff nearby at all times. It seemed like an odd quirk to me, but I didn't care, because its relative isolation meant that I was unlikely to be seen by a lot of people.

Landing in the driveway, I walked up to the front gates, where two large men carrying heavy-looking guns stood. They looked like mansion security, but as far as I could tell, neither of them were superhumans. They were just regular old humans with big guns, though I knew how hard it could be to identify a superhuman if you didn't know that they had powers.

The two men stiffened when they saw me approaching. They didn't point their guns at me, but I saw their fingers itching to pull the triggers. I could dodge the bullets if I had to—super speed and all—but I still wished I had my old suit, because it was bullet-proof and would have provided me with more defense against their weapons.

"Who are you, kid?" said one of the security guards, looking down at me with a sneer. "Lost? Or do you need us to call your parents to drive you home?"

I was actually kind of amazed that the guard didn't seem shocked to see me fly in, but I rolled with it. "I'm Bolt. I have a meeting with your boss tonight. He invited me, so you need to let me inside so I'm not late."

"Bolt?" said the security guard. "Like the superhero? You don't look like him. Where's your suit?"

"Not available at the moment," I said. "But why don't you call up your boss and confirm that I have a meeting scheduled with him for this evening?"

"Why should we listen to *you*?" said the second guard. "You're just a stupid kid claiming to be a superhero. Mr. Plutarch doesn't have time for—"

I didn't even let him finish his sentence. I zipped over to him, ripped his gun out of his hand, and then snapped it over my knee, tossing aside the two halves before zipping back over to where I was standing moments before. Both guards stared at me in shock.

"There," I said. "Is that proof enough for you or would you prefer more *personal* proof?"

The two guards exchanged looks before the first guard grabbed the walkie talkie on his shoulder and, speaking into it, said, "We've got a kid here saying he's the superhero Bolt and he's got a meeting with Mr. Plutarch. Can you confirm that?"

Static crackled as a voice on the other end said, "Confirmed. Mr. Plutarch has a meeting with someone named Bolt for six o'clock this evening. You may let him in."

The guard didn't look happy that I was right, but he must have still remembered how I broke his friend's gun, because he just said, "Affirmative," and stepped aside as the gates opened. I walked past both of the guards, feeling their glares at me, but I didn't look at either of them as I entered the mansion's courtyard.

Upon reaching the front door, I almost knocked on it when the door suddenly opened and I found myself face-to-face with an elderly British gentleman I had never seen before. He was tall and thin, very much like the stereotypical British butler. He had a severe look to him, which made me not want to anger him, even though I could probably break him in half without even thinking about it.

"Hi," I said, putting on a friendly smile. "I'm Bolt. I'm here for my meeting with Plutarch."

The butler didn't say anything at first, which made me wonder if I had accidentally said something wrong or if the butler thought there was something suspicious about me. For some reason I expected him to attack me, maybe because I was still remembering what Triplet had told me about his suspicions about Plutarch's real plans.

Then he nodded and said, in a Southern drawl, “Well, Mr. Bolt, why don't you come in and get a seat? Master Plutarch is already waiting for ya in the living room.”

I blinked. I hadn't expected him to have a Southern accent. He looked incredibly British, but he spoke like a good old boy of the South.

But I just said, “He is?”

“Certainly,” said the butler. He stepped aside. “Come on in, now, and let me show you to the living room, where the master is.”

Sensing nothing wrong, I walked through the doorway and into the fanciest entryway I had ever seen. It was wide-open and almost sparkling clean, with a golden statue of a man who looked very much like Plutarch (excerpt wearing colonial clothing) posed in the center, which I assumed was a statue of some famous ancestor of Plutarch or something. Two wide staircases led from the floor up to the second floor, but the butler didn't lead me up those.

Instead, he took me to the room behind the statue, which seemed to be the living room. It was enormous, about the size of my entire house. The walls and ceiling had shiny white tiles, while the floor was covered in a shag carpet that felt like a fluffy pillow. It even smelled fancy, like caviar or something. A gigantic flat screen TV—three times as big as the one in the House—stood on one end of the room, with a huge sound system hooked up to it and a large set of fancy-looking sofas situated in front of it. A large window, with a nook for reading, revealed the fantastic garden on the other side behind the house.

Reclining in an armchair that looked more expensive than Dad's car was Plutarch himself. He was dressed in fancy red robes, reading a huge book that I didn't recognize. He looked up when we entered and smiled that same grin he had shown me when we first met back in Fallsville.

“Master Plutarch,” said the butler as we stopped a few feet from Plutarch. He gestured at me. “This is Mr. Bolt, the young man you wanted to meet. He's here for your six o'clock meeting.”

“That's him?” said Plutarch. He looked at me with skepticism. “What happened to your suit, kid?”

“It just … isn't available right now,” I said, hoping to steer the conversation away from my costume. “This is the best I could do with what I had.”

Plutarch chuckled. “Resourceful! That's good. Too many kids nowadays just don't know how to use what they have. You're smart. That's what I like about you.”

I felt a little embarrassed at Plutarch's praise, while the butler said, “Don't worry, sir. This young man is the same Bolt who saved you from that metal-skinned fella a couple of weeks ago. I confirmed it.”

“Good to know,” said Plutarch. He gestured in the other direction. “You can leave now, Jack. If we need anything, I'll let you know.”

The butler—whose name was apparently Jack—nodded, turned around, and left the living room, leaving me all alone with Plutarch, who shut his book closed and put it on the stand next to his seat. That was when I noticed the book's cover, which had a big picture of Plutarch's face, with a serious expression, on it, with the title *The Science of Negotiation* written above it and Plutarch's own name at the bottom.

"Um," I said. "Jack said he confirmed my identity. But how? It's not like I have an ID to confirm my superhero identity or anything."

"Oh, Jack is a superhuman," said Plutarch as he steepled his fingers together. "He's basically a living lie detector. He probably used his power on you to find out if you were lying about your identity or not. He's a great guy, been my butler for years."

I nodded, remembering what Triplet had told me about the superhumans that Plutarch hired. I hoped that Jack was the only one at this mansion, because if I had to fight, I figured I'd rather fight a living lie detector than someone with steel skin or capable of throwing fireballs.

"Take a seat, kid," said Plutarch, gesturing at the other recliner opposite him. "No need to stand."

Feeling a little awkward at Plutarch's generosity, I nonetheless sat down on the recliner, which I practically sank into. It was the softest and most comfortable chair I had ever sat in in my whole life. I reclined into it, becoming so comfortable that I almost forgot the whole reason I was even here.

"Like it?" said Plutarch. "It's a Plutarch brand chair. Made out of only the finest and softest materials in the world. Very expensive."

"Yeah," I said, feeling a little sleepy. "I feel like I could just fall asleep …"

"But you won't," said Plutarch. He leaned forward, a serious look on his face. "We're going to talk, remember?"

I shook my head to get rid of the sleepiness and then sat up, but it was hard because I kept sinking into the seat. I did my best to focus, however.

"Yes," I said, nodding. "I remember. Though I'm surprised that you wanted to speak with me, considering how unimportant I am."

Plutarch chuckled. "Unimportant? Kid, I'm a huge fan of yours. You're pretty well-known for defeating Master Chaos, after all. Old bastard got what was coming to him."

"Did you know Master Chaos?" I said.

"Back when I was, ah, less honest, we crossed paths a couple of times," said Plutarch. He shook his head. "Always seemed too crazy to me. Didn't really have any business sense. Liked big, dramatic plans. Not like mine, though. Mine were more subtle and practical."

'Plutarch' and 'subtle' didn't seem to go together to me, but maybe I was overlooking something. Maybe that was a clue that Plutarch was up to something, but I did not say that aloud. "Did you two ever work together?"

"Nope," said Plutarch, shaking his head. "We never got along and actually fought a few times whenever our plans crossed. But anyway, what's past is past. I built Plutarch Industries by looking at the future, not by obsessing over the past."

I nodded, although it didn't surprise me that Plutarch hadn't worked with Master Chaos. Chaos had not seemed like the kind of villain to work with anyone except his family. Still, I made a mental note to check Neo Ranks later anyway, just to make sure Plutarch wasn't lying to me.

"So what did you want to talk about?" said Plutarch. He

glanced at his watch. "Let's be quick about this, because I have a flight to catch in about an hour to do some campaigning in New Mexico tomorrow."

I almost asked outright, 'Sir, are you running for President on an anti-neohero platform in order to become America's first dictator?' but I caught myself before I asked that question, mostly because I knew that there was no way that Plutarch would give me an honest answer.

Instead, I said, "I wanted to talk with you about the Vile Four."

Plutarch's friendly smile suddenly vanished, replaced by an angry scowl that made me feel afraid. "What about those idiots? And I include myself in that, by the way, because I regret ever working with those morons."

"It's just that I noticed that the former members of the team have been active again," I said. "I fought both Steel Skin and Firespirit, who tried to kill you and Sagan. I just—"

"If you're going to accuse me of working with them, think again," said Plutarch. He looked at the burning fire in the fireplace between us. "I haven't spoken with any of those idiots since I helped put them in jail years ago. Well, okay, I 'spoke' to Steel Skin when he attacked me, but beyond that, I don't know anything about what they're doing or planning."

"I didn't say you did," I said. "I just wanted your thoughts on them."

Plutarch chuckled. "I know the rumors, kid. I have a dozen staffers on the Internet all day just following the rumors about me. I know that a lot of people don't think I've *really* reformed, that I'm just a liar. I've had to deal with those rumors for years, but I guess they haven't stopped me from winning the nomination of my party, have they?"

Plutarch sounded satisfied with that, like he had had the last laugh against his opponents and critics. He even chuckled, though I didn't find it amusing myself.

"So you don't know anything about Steel Skin or Firespirit or even Nail Gun?" I said.

"Nothing," said Plutarch. He looked at me again. "I might be one of the richest men in the world, but that doesn't mean I keep track of every person I've ever associated with. Especially those three idiots, who weren't even good minions when they worked for me."

"I see," I said. It was hard to tell if Plutarch was lying or not, but it seemed to me like he wasn't. "Then why did you bail them out of Ultimate Max?"

Plutarch suddenly looked worried for a moment before his usual confident grin returned. "Where did you hear that?"

"From Neo Ranks," I said. "It's a website about neoheroes and stuff. It also has news and information about supervillains, both current and retired."

"It's a lie," Plutarch said. "I would never bail them out for any reason. I have much better things to spend my money on, like attack ads against crazy Barney."

"But if you didn't bail them out, then who did?" I said. "And why was it reported on Neo Ranks that you did it?"

"I don't know who did it, but I imagine it was someone who is trying to sabotage my campaign," said Plutarch. "Bet it was one of the NHA guys. They hate me and would do anything to make sure that I don't win the election and 'destroy' America."

"So it was just a coincidence, then, that Firespirit tried to take out Sagan, who is your primary rival for the presidency?" I said.

"Complete and utter coincidence," said Plutarch. "In fact, as soon as I heard about the assassination, I sent out a press release condemning it. Because see, I play fair, unlike some people, and I'd never hire an assassin to kill anyone, even someone I'm running against in a major election like this."

I hadn't heard about the press release, but I decide to keep pressing forward. "Do you have any idea who might have done it?"

"None," said Plutarch. "But good work stopping Firespirit, by the way. He always annoyed me more than Steel Skin or Nail Gun because he thought he was some kind of 'Spirit of Flame' or whatever. Kept trying to overthrow me whenever I wasn't looking. Now that I think about, I'm not sure why I didn't just have someone kill him whenever he failed to overthrow me." Plutarch shrugged. "Guess I was a good guy even in my old villain days."

"Oh, I didn't beat Firespirit on my own," I said, scratching the back of my head in embarrassment. "Incantation and the other Young Neos helped, too."

"Incantation, huh?" said Plutarch. He sounded even less jovial than before. "She's Thaumaturge's apprentice, right? The girl who helped you defeat and capture Steel Skin?"

"Yeah," I said. "You've met her before."

"I remember," said Plutarch. He shook his head. "Though I wish I hadn't. She's every bit as stuck up as her master, if not worse."

"You've met Thaumaturge?" I said in curiosity.

"Oh, yeah," said Plutarch. "Back when I was the Billionaire, I met lots of neoheroes who got in the way of my master plans. I always clashed with Thaumaturge more than the others, though, which is why I don't care much for his apprentice."

Plutarch shook his head. He pulled a cigar out of his robes, lit it, and started puffing on it. "But I don't need their support or approval. All I need to do is convince the American people to vote for me and I'm gold. Those two can just go and pull rabbits out of hats at children's magic shows for all I care."

"I guess you have a similar relationship with other heroes," I said. "Like Genius."

"You mean your dad?" said Plutarch. He scowled. "Oh, yeah. He was always too smart for his own good. He was so smart that I tried to hire him to work at Plutarch Industries as a weapons developer after he thwarted one of my plans, but he just told to take that six-figure salary and shove it up my you-know-where."

"Dad never told me that," I said.

"Of course he wouldn't," said Plutarch. "But I always respected Genius anyway. Always independent and resourceful, two traits I can respect in anyone regardless of whether they're friend or foe."

"Is that why you like me?" I said. "Is it because I'm Genius's son?"

"That plays into it," said Plutarch. "Even though you're a neohero, I can tell you're a good kid at heart. I don't know if you can vote yet or not, but it doesn't matter. I trust good kids and that's what you are."

Plutarch seemed sincere. In fact, he was so sincere that I was starting to feel ashamed of ever suspecting him of being up to no good in the first place.

So I said, "Thanks, Mr. Plutarch. But I'm still a neohero. Doesn't that affect your opinion of me at all?"

"It would if you were one of my haters," said Plutarch. He removed his cigar from his mouth and blew some smoke. "But really, I don't care. One of the promises I've made to the American people is that I will pass laws forcing neoheroes to pay for whatever collateral damage their battles cause."

"I know," I said. "I've heard people complaining about it."

"It's always neoheroes who complain about it," Plutarch pointed out. "But they never realized just how much money we lose every year just to their fights with the various supervillains. I'm talking about losses in the billions here, often paid for by the taxpayer. So I'm going to change that, no matter what your fellow neoheroes say."

"That doesn't sound too bad," I said. "It seems almost like common sense to me."

"Exactly, but common sense ain't so common nowadays," said Plutarch. He lowered his cigar and sighed, "Sad."

I could tell that this conversation was coming to a close. I didn't really care much for whatever Plutarch's policies were. He didn't seem to be planning to do anything evil, but maybe he was just hiding it. In any case, I decided to let Triplet keep investigating him, because I needed to get home quickly before it got too late and my parents wondered why I was late.

So I stood up and said, "Thanks for the talk, Mr. Plutarch. You answered my questions, so I'm going to leave and go back home now."

"Sure," said Plutarch. "But I have a quick question that I hope you can answer for me."

I tilted my head to the side. "What is that?"

"Can you endorse me at my next rally?" said Plutarch, without missing a beat.

"Endorse you?" I said. "Why?"

"Because I need a young, well-known neohero like you to endorse me and help me win the youth vote," said Plutarch. "An endorsement from a neohero like you wouldn't give me a huge boost, but it would probably be enough to help me beat crazy Barney in the election, especially since it is so close."

I was about to say that I didn't care one way or another about who became President when I noticed movement outside the window. I looked over, but saw nothing in the garden outside, which made me think that I had seen a bird or something fly by when something smashed through the window and landed on the floor.

"What the hell?" said Plutarch, rising to his feet and looking over at the thing that had broken through the window. "What was that?"

I didn't answer. I looked at the thing on the floor and saw that it was a sphere. I thought it was just a rock at first, but then I heard a tiny beep from it and I, instantly realizing what that was, said, "Mr. Plutarch, get down!"

I grabbed Plutarch and shoved him to the floor. Then I fell down on top of him just as the bomb exploded.

CHAPTER ELEVEN

I FELT THE HEAT and flames from the exploding bomb behind me, but did not look over my shoulder at it in order to save my face. I was trying to keep Plutarch—who had become a quivering mess under me—safe from the explosion, even though my hodgepodge of a costume was probably not good against fire. The volume of the explosion was the worst part, however, because I was practically deafened by the noise it made.

But eventually, the explosion faded. Hesitantly, I looked over my shoulder to see the damage.

The living room looked like it had been completely nuked. The flat screen TV had been almost completely melted, while the sofas were on fire or burnt to a crisp. What remained of the main window had been shattered, while the curtains were nothing more than smoking remains. Oddly, there were nails embedded in almost everything; in fact, there were so many nails that I wondered how we had managed to avoid them. My clothes, thankfully, were still in one piece, although I noticed a few holes in the back of my hoodie that smoked slightly.

Standing up, I looked around carefully, but did not see anyone who might have thrown the bomb. At least until someone jumped through the smashed window and landed in the crater created by the bomb.

The guy who jumped through the window looked crazy. He wore homemade metal armor and carried a really weird-looking gun that didn't seem to fire bullets. And on top of his bald head was a hard hat, although I doubted this guy was here to do any construction.

"Did it work?" said the guy, looking around the room eagerly. "Is he—"

He cut himself off as soon as he saw me and Plutarch and scowled. "Damn it. How did you survive?"

I wasn't sure who this guy was until Plutarch, who was now crouched behind me, said, "Nail Gun? What are you doing here?"

"Why, I am here to kill you, of course," said Nail Gun. He pointed his gun at me. "I don't know who the kid is, but I'll kill him, too, while I'm at it."

Nail Gun? That was one of the former members of the Vile Four. I took a fighting stance and said, "Kill me? Good luck with that. I'm not just a kid. I'm a neohero."

"So? Neoheroes can still be killed," said Nail Gun. He waved his gun. "Especially with my nail gun, which I designed specially to kill neoheroes like you."

"Where's security?" said Plutarch, looking at the entrance to the living room. "They should have caught you before you even thought about entering."

"They did, but I killed them before they could catch me," said Nail Gun with a crazed grin. "I disabled your security systems, too, so no one else knows that we're here. And by the time anyone finds out that I killed you … well, there won't be enough of you left to cremate."

"Stay back, Mr. Plutarch," I said, holding my hand toward Plutarch behind me. "I'll distract Nail Gun. You should leave and call the police."

"Oh, no you don't!" Nail Gun yelled.

Suddenly, nails started shooting out of Nail Gun's gun. I grabbed a nearby chair and held it in front of us, catching the bullets in the chair's soft upholstery. They hit like actual bullets, but thankfully the chair was thick enough to catch them.

Then I heard something fly through the air and in a second another nail bomb flew over the chair and landed on the floor behind us. Alarmed, I lashed out and kicked the nail bomb as hard as I could, sending it flying so fast that it broke through the wall and exploded on the other side, sparing us from getting blown to bits.

Then I tossed the nail-studded chair at Nail Gun, but the villain dodged it by rolling to the side. The recliner crashed into the ground just as Nail Gun aimed his gun at us again.

But this time, I activated my super speed and zoomed over to him. Before Nail Gun could even realize what was happening, I snatched his gun from his hand and threw it away. But Nail Gun immediately pulled out a long, rusty nail from his armor and tried to stab me with it, though I dodged it easily and punched Nail Gun in the face.

Or tried to, but Nail Gun dodged my fist at the last possible minute. My punch went wide, leaving my stomach unprotected. A second later, I felt something thick and hard pierce my abdomen, followed by a rush of hot blood that made me shout in pain. I lashed out wildly, but Nail Gun dodged it easily and then, yanking his nail out of my side, kicked me in the side with his foot, which was covered in a thick, steel-toed boot.

Damn it, the pain hurt. I fell to the floor with a gasp, feeling the blood leaking out of my wound. I had taken some serious hits before, but this hurt more than any other. The pain was so overwhelming that I could barely think. I was conscious enough, however, to notice Nail Gun step over me, probably making his way to Plutarch, but I couldn't ignore the pain long enough to even sit up.

Gritting my teeth, I heard Nail Gun pick up his gun off the floor nearby. I also heard him start to walk over to Plutarch, but I couldn't let him do that.

Doing my best to ignore the pain in my side, I rolled over onto my other side and grabbed Nail Gun's boot. I looked up at him through tears in my eyes, blinking hard, while he looked back at me over his shoulder with surprise.

"You're still conscious?" said Nail Gun.

"No …" Each word was impossible to get out. "Don't … kill … Plutarch …"

"Dumb kid," said Nail Gun. He aimed his gun at me. "Why don't you let the adults talk?"

There was no way I could dodge Nail Gun's gun. I just stared up at it, trying to gather the strength to knock him down, but I had lost too much blood and was in too much pain to even try to pull him down. I hoped, at least, that my death would be quick and painless.

But then, all of a sudden, a large book came out of nowhere and struck Nail Gun in the back of the head. Nail Gun yelped in pain, staggering to the side as Plutarch—wielding *The Science of Negotiation*—appeared. He swung the book at Nail Gun's hand, knocking the weapon out of it and making Nail Gun jerk his hand back with a howl of pain.

Plutarch caught the gun before it hit the floor and aimed it at Nail Gun. Nail Gun immediately raised his hands in surrender, a look of fear on his face.

"Hey, Adam, let's not be hasty now," said Nail Gun. All of his confidence and composure from earlier had been replaced with a cowardly, trembling tone. "There's no need to shoot me, you know. If you just want to call the police to take me in, I'd go as quietly as a mouse. I'll even take off my armor if that's what you want."

Plutarch snorted. "You haven't changed at all, Nathan. Acting all tough and manly when you are in charge, but then turning into a groveling nitwit when the tables turn on you. Now I remember why you were always my *least* favorite minion. Annoying."

"So will you spare me anyway?" said Nail Gun with a gulp. "After all, only supervillains ever kill their enemies in cold blood and you are no supervillain anymore. Therefore, you should be much more merci—"

A click of the gun's trigger and a nail struck Nail Gun in the head. Nail Gun immediately collapsed, blood leaking from the spot where the nail had sunk.

Plutarch lowered the nail gun, a look of pure disgust on his face. "Just because I'm not a villain anymore doesn't mean I'm a hero."

I stared at the dead Nail Gun with a mixture of relief and horror, but then I remembered I was still bleeding to death. I gasped in pain, putting my hands over the bloody wound, while Plutarch looked down at me.

"You okay, kid?" said Plutarch, kneeling over me, the nail gun still in his hand. "Do you need a doctor?"

"Y-Yes," I said. My consciousness was fading in and out. "Please call one right … right away …"

I couldn't handle the pain and blood loss anymore. Everything went black and I thought no more.

CHAPTER TWELVE

MY HEAD. FOR SOME reason my head hurt. I didn't know why. I just knew that there was a dull, throbbing pain, a pain that I could barely tolerate. Ow, ow, ow … god damn.

Not only that, but people were talking nearby. They spoke quietly, but even their low tones made my head hurt. I tried to open my eyes, but it was hard, like they had been taped shut.

Nonetheless, I eventually managed to crack my eye open wide enough to see that I was lying on a soft bed, with a white sheet pulled over my body. I blinked, trying to figure out where I was, but my senses felt like they had been knocked out and were slowly coming back to normal again.

That was when I noticed that I was not alone. Two people sat in chairs next to my bed, two people I didn't recognize at first. I blinked a couple of times to clear my vision and saw that they were Incantation and Hopper, of all people. They sat by my bed, practically whispering to each other, leaving me unable to understand what they were saying. I thought I heard my name—my superhero name—mentioned, but that was all I could discern.

I needed to know how I had gotten here; for that matter, I needed to know where 'here' was. I tilted my head toward them and said, in a weak voice, “Hello?”

I didn't say that very loudly, but Incantation and Hopper jumped when they heard me nonetheless. They looked at me with concern and Incantation even leaned toward me a little like she was worried about me.

“Bolt?” said Incantation. “How do you feel?”

“Like a rock,” I said. I groaned. “Where am I?”

“The House,” said Incantation. “You're at our on-base medical station. This is where we get our injuries healed.”

“The House?” I said. My throat was dry, but I kept talking anyway. “Not a hospital?”

“Nope,” said Hopper, shaking his head. “Can't trust hospitals. Doctors and nurses tend to be very nosy people, if you catch my drift. They'd probably unmask you if we brought you there.”

I raised my hand and touched my face, feeling the ski mask that still covered it. I sighed in relief. “So no one removed my mask?”

“No one,” Hopper confirmed. “Though we had to remove your shirt to fix your stab wound.”

I felt the spot on my body where I had been stabbed. I winced slightly when I felt a bandaged area, but it was not bloody and the pain had gone down quite a bit.

I looked at them again. “Who fixed me?”

“Technical,” said Hopper. “Not only is she a tech whiz, but she's also a budding surgeon. She got you fixed up no problem.”

“So I'll be okay?” I said.

“As long as you rest,” said Incantation. “Do you need some

water? You sound thirsty."

"Yes, please," I said.

Incantation stood up and hovered away, while I looked around the room I was lying in. It was a medium-sized, white room that looked like the kind of room you'd find in a fancy hospital. My hoodie hung on a coat hanger near the door, while some potted plants stood in the corner. There was also a sink, where Incantation filled up a cup for me and then walked back over to my side.

I took the cup of water and started drinking. The cool liquid felt good on my parched lips and I didn't stop until I drank it all.

Then, lowering the cup, I said, "Ah, that was good. Thanks."

"No problem," said Incantation. "So where is your suit?"

I rubbed my head. "My dad took it from me. He didn't like the fact that I had lied to him about where I was going, so he took my costume away and won't give it back to me until after graduation."

"Aw, man," said Hopper, snapping his fingers. "And you just let him take it?"

"What could I do?" I said with a shrug. "He's my dad. But anyway, how long have I been out? What time is it?"

"It's noon on Saturday," said Incantation. "You were out all night."

"Do my parents know where I am?" I said.

"We don't know where your parents are, so we couldn't contact them," said Incantation. "But who cares, really? What matters is that this is the safest place for you at the moment, so you don't need to worry about anything right now."

"What about Plutarch and Nail Gun?" I said. "I remember

Plutarch killed him. What happened after that?"

"Plutarch called the police," said Hopper. He said Plutarch's name like it was an insult. "He tried to stop us from saving you, but he's still an old man and was too slow to keep us from taking you through one of my portals."

"You didn't hurt him, did you?" I said.

"No, but we did warn him not to mess with us," said Incantation. Her hands balled into fists. "I would have loved to hurt him, though. That bastard deserves it, considering all of the bad things he's done."

"Why were you even at his mansion in the first place?" said Hopper in disgust. "Why would *any* self-respecting neohero be at his mansion?"

"I was trying to find out whether Plutarch was behind the attacks from the former members of the Vile Four," I said. "That's why."

"Well, what did you find out?" said Incantation.

"He said he has nothing to do with them," I said. "He told me that he didn't bail them out of jail, but he didn't know who actually did."

"Right," said Incantation. She rolled her eyes. "Of course Plutarch didn't bail out his former minions. Why would he? It's not like he has worked with them in the past or anything."

"But if they're working for him, why did Nail Gun and Steel Skin try to kill him?" I said. "It makes no sense."

"It's probably just a trick," said Incantation, shaking her head. "Plutarch was known for creating complex schemes and committing crimes that were impossible to trace back to him. He probably lied to you as a way to throw you off his trail."

"That's exactly the sort of thing he'd do," said Hopper, nodding seriously. "He's so icky and gross. I'm glad we don't have anything to do with him."

"He seems sane to me," I said, "but I guess he could have been lying."

"He was," Incantation said. "He absolutely was. We can't prove it yet, but one of these days we will. Of course, it might not matter if Senator Sagan wins the election next month, because that by itself would ruin whatever Plutarch is planning."

I rubbed the back of my head and said, "So how did you guys even find me? I didn't tell anyone that I was going to meet him."

"We received a report that Nail Gun was attacking Plutarch's mansion," said Incantation. She gestured at herself and Hopper. "We've been tasked with keeping an eye on the Vile Four in case they attempt to mess with the election. So when Nail Gun attacked, Technical's drones sent us a message about it."

"Yeah," said Hopper. "We didn't even know you were there until we arrived and saw you bleeding out like that. We almost thought you were dead until we noticed you were breathing."

"Well, I'm glad you showed up anyway," I said. "I really thought I was a goner back there. I just wish Plutarch hadn't killed Nail Gun, though."

"Why?" said Incantation. "As much as I hate Plutarch, I have to admit that he did the right thing there. Nail Gun was a bad guy."

"Because I hoped we could capture him and interrogate him to find out who hired him and Firespirit and possibly Steel Skin, too," I said.

"He was working for Plutarch," said Hopper. "Probably

Plutarch killed him so that no one would know. I mean, if the police caught Nail Gun and he confessed to working for Plutarch, that alone would completely destroy his campaign even among his most diehard supporters."

"Right," I said, "but I'm still not sure about it. Something doesn't add up. Like a piece of a much larger puzzle is missing."

"The only thing that is missing is definitive proof of Plutarch's connection to the Vile Four," said Incantation. "Or should I say, the Vile Three, because Plutarch was the fourth member who never went to jail for his crimes."

"Maybe," I said. I sat up in the bed and stretched my arms, trying to get the tiredness out of them. "Has anything else happened since you guys took me here?"

"Not that we know of," said Incantation. "All I know is that Nail Gun's body is going to be given back to his family and that they will likely give him a funeral sometime soon. There won't be any charges filed against Plutarch, either, due to the fact that he killed Nail Gun in self-defense."

"So Sagan didn't say anything?" I said.

"Why should he?" said Hopper. "Plutarch is always attacking Sagan, so why should Sagan comment on Nail Gun's attack? Besides, Sagan probably hasn't had enough time to respond, so if he does have a response, it won't be until later."

"Right," I said. I rolled my shoulders. "Anyway, I think I'll be leaving soon. I'm not looking forward to talking to my parents, because they're probably going to be very angry with me, but I don't want them worrying about where I am or how I'm doing, either."

Incantation suddenly stood up. "No. You should stay and rest.

You are still recovering from your injury and shouldn't be going anywhere until tomorrow at leas."

I felt my bandaged wound gingerly. "It doesn't feel that bad. Besides, I'm not planning to get into another fight. I just want to recover in my own bed back home."

I sat up straighter, but then Incantation suddenly shoved me back down. She wasn't particularly strong, but her sudden movement took me by surprise. She then pulled her hands away from my chest, looking down at me with her green eyes.

"I said, you will *stay* put," said Incantation. "Stay. Understand?"

I was about to say that no, I didn't understand, and that I didn't really need to understand, but then I felt something in my head move a little. It felt like someone was putting pressure on my mind, a familiar sensation, but I wasn't sure where I had felt it before.

The sensation faded quickly, though, so I said, "Okay, I'll stay. How long?"

"For as long as it takes you to recover," said Incantation. "And by the time you do, you'll be a completely different person."

"What?" I said. "What do you mean, I'll be a completely different person?"

Instead of answering my question, Incantation waved her hand at me. "It's nothing. Just rest. You look tired."

I was about to say that no, I didn't, but then a sudden drowsiness came over me. I sank into my sheets and mattresses, fighting to keep my eyes open, but my eye lids were just too heavy, like heavy curtains being drawn over my eyes.

The last thing I saw, before I went under completely, was

Incantation's smirking face.

I awoke again, but I wasn't sure how much later. I thought about going back to sleep, because it was really dark, but then I noticed that I wasn't lying in my bed anymore. Instead, I was lying on cold, hard concrete, clad in my makeshift super suit. I touched my face and felt my ski mask, which still clung to my head.

My head didn't hurt anymore, though my wound was still bandaged. I slowly but surely sat up, doing my best not to reopen my wound, and looked around the room. It was too dark to see anything; I couldn't even see my hands in front of my face.

"Hello?" I called out. "Is anyone there?"

My words echoed off into the distance, which made me wonder if I was stuck at the bottom of a pit. That didn't make any sense, though, because I had been lying in a hospital bed just moments ago.

Or had it been moments ago? I didn't know how much time had actually passed. It didn't feel like a lot of time had passed, but how could I be sure? There wasn't even a wall clock for me to check.

Rising to my feet, I said, "Incantation? Hopper? Is anyone there?"

No answer. Just my own words echoing back at me, until they eventually faded into nothingness.

Then I heard footsteps somewhere in the darkness. I looked around, but the echoing made it impossible to tell which direction the footsteps were coming from. My survival instinct kicked in, however, so I summoned my super strength, ready to fight if necessary.

A light suddenly turned on, which made me cover my eyes for a moment to avoid getting blinded. But eventually, my eyes adjusted to the bright light and I lowered my hands to see what had caused it.

Sarah Jane Watson stood there, carrying a large, bulky flashlight in her hand. Although she looked pretty much the same as she did before, she no longer looked nearly as frightened or timid. She was smiling, the first time I had ever seen her smile, and it was the creepiest smile I had ever seen in my life. Some girls, when they smiled, looked beautiful, but with Sarah, it actually made her look even uglier than ever.

"Sarah?" I said. "What are you doing here? Where am I? Where are the others?"

Sarah just kept smiling. "The others are safe. But they aren't important at the moment. What is important is fixing your mind."

I frowned. "What? My mind is fine, thank you very much. Is this a joke?"

"A joke?" said Sarah indignantly. "This isn't a joke. This is super serious, but I guess a gross guy like you wouldn't understand."

"Listen, Sarah, I don't have time for your games," I said. "I just need to find out where I am and how to get out of here. My parents are probably worried sick about me."

"Who cares what your parents think?" said Sarah derisively. "They probably believe all that crap about super powers being genetic and other problematic things. So gross and wrong."

"But it's true," I said. "Super powers are genetic and—"

Suddenly, I heard a loud, crashing sound like hundreds of pots and pans being banged together over and over again. I slammed my hands over my ears, but I still heard the crashing sounds as clearly as ever, like the noise was inside my head. The noises actually sounded like screaming voices, like someone had recorded a bunch of other people screaming and then remixed the sound into something monstrous and deafening.

I fell to my knees, trying to block out the crashing and screaming, but it didn't work. I looked up at Sarah, who appeared entirely unaffected by the loud noises that came from everywhere.

"Sarah, what's going on?" I shouted, my voice lost in the crashing and screaming. "Is this your doing?"

Sarah didn't answer. She just looked at me coldly, like I should know what was going on. I felt like my head was about to explode.

But then Sarah waved her hand and the crashing and screaming stopped just as suddenly as it came. I was never one for silence, but the silence that followed was pure bliss in comparison to the agonizing sounds that had assaulted my mind just moments earlier.

But I still didn't rise. I lowered my hands from my ears hesitatingly and then looked around again, but I didn't see yje source of the sounds anywhere.

"There," said Sarah. "That is what you get for daring to say such gross things to me."

Rubbing the back of my head, I looked up at Sarah and said, "What is going on? Where are we? Is this your doing?"

"Oh my god, you just keep asking the same questions over and over," said Sarah with a sigh. "It's so problematic. You should educate yourself."

"Educate myself?" I said in disbelief. "How? I don't even know where to start."

"I guess I'll have to tell you, then," said Sarah with a long, annoyed sigh. "Whatever. I doubt you'll listen, because you genetics types tend to be really arrogant and gross, but whatever."

"Just get on with it," I said. "Are we still in the House?"

"Yes," said Sarah. "I won't tell you exactly where, however, because you aren't supposed to know that. All you need to know is that you're stuck here for good."

"What is the purpose of this place, then?" I said. "Why am I down here? Is this some kind of test?"

"Test? I hate tests," said Sarah. "No, actually we're just going to … correct some of your problematic ideas."

"Problematic ideas?" I said. "What do you mean?"

"Like, educate you," said Sarah. "We're going to make sure that you stop being such an oppressive, mean person. We're going to make you better so that when we let you back out, you won't go around spouting such harmful things anymore."

"I don't need any education," I said. I rose back to my feet again, but this time I was ready to run if I had to. "I'm fine just the way I am."

"No, you're not," said Sarah. She shuddered, like I had just said something extremely offensive. "You just don't know how ignorant you are."

"Well, if you're going to give me an education, this is a pretty silly classroom," I said, looking around the area. "There aren't even any blackboards."

"That's not the kind of education we're going to give you," said Sarah. "We're going to give you the kind of education you *need*, even though you obviously don't think that you do."

"Why?" I said. "Why not just let me go?"

"Because we're not supposed to," said Sarah. "We were told to make you into one of us."

"Who told you that?" I said. "Someone in the NHA?"

"I'm not telling you that," said Sarah, shaking her head. "All you need to know is that we are going to make you one of us … whether you want to or not."

"What if I don't want to become one of you?" I said. I stepped backwards. "What if I want to go home and never speak with you or your freak friends ever again?"

Sarah suddenly burst into tears. "Freak friends? That's so harmful. You're such a mean person."

"No, I'm not," I said. "I'm—"

I was interrupted by the screaming and crashing sounds again, which forced me back down to my knees. I covered my ears, but the sounds echoed in my skull, crashing again and again against my thoughts. I tried screaming, but my jaw felt wired shut.

"Stop thinking," said Sarah. Her voice sounded clear in my head, despite the screaming and crashing sounds. "Stop disagreeing. Only obey. Only listen. Never question."

I would have told Sarah what she could do with herself, but the mental pounding I was taking was too much. I tried standing, activating my super strength to make me strong, but even with my power flowing through me, I could barely stand. I took a step toward Sarah, but it seemed like Sarah was a million miles away, even though she couldn't have been more than fifty feet away, if that.

"Lie down," said Sarah. "I can end the pain if you would just stop questioning. If you agree to accept the truth, then I can help you."

"What … truth?" I said. Even just saying those two words was almost impossible.

"That our powers are nothing more than a social construct," said Sarah, "that if we are to achieve *true* equality, that we must be inclusive of everyone and never question another's identity regardless of what the 'facts' say."

I bit my lower lip. The screaming and crashing sounds were intensely painful, but I'd never agree to that. Still, I needed to stop Sarah. I wasn't sure if she actually had powers and the others had lied to me earlier when they said she didn't or if this was part of some weird technology or something. All I knew was that I would go insane if I didn't stop it as soon as possible.

So I activated my super speed and ran straight at her. I didn't intend to kill or even harm her, but if I could stop her, that would be good.

But then I ran straight through her, like she didn't really exist at all. Skidding to a stop, I turned to face Sarah, who was now flickering in and out of existence like a hologram.

Sarah turned to face me, her smirk never leaving her lips. "So stupid. Did you really think I'd be here in person, where you could harm me? Of course not. Doing things in person is icky anyway. I like to do things where I'm safe from harm."

"Then where …" I stopped speaking when the sounds in my head temporarily increased in volume, but then forced myself to keep speaking anyway. "Then where are you?"

"I'm not going to tell you," said Sarah. "At least not until you listen and believe, anyway. Will you?"

I shook my head. “Never. I don't know what's really going on here, but I'm going to leave whether you want me to or not.”

“That's what others have said,” said Sarah. “But they always break at some point or another. It's just a matter of finding the right pressure.”

All of a sudden, the screaming and crashing sounds in my head grew deafeningly loud. I couldn't even hear my own thoughts. It was like a bomb had gone off in my head. I screamed in agony and fell down to my hands and knees, only this time I wasn't sure I would be getting up again. It felt like a giant hand was pressing down on me, pushing me down harder and harder despite myself.

I tried to scream. I tried to yell. I tried to fight it. But this wasn't a physical thing like a robot. It was mental and I didn't have any mental powers. I couldn't fight against it. I dug my fingers into the floor, praying that my pain would leave, but it did nothing.

“At what point will you break?” Sarah said above me, her voice still clear. “But you know, we don't *have* to break you. If you would just agree to be reeducated, we could skip all this. I hate having to harm you like this, but this is what we have to do sometimes when dealing with problematic people like you.”

What a liar. I could tell, even in my pain, that Sarah was taking great joy in watching me suffer. She was enjoying every moment of this, taking glee in my pain. I wanted to strangle her, but I couldn't.

“We can end this anytime,” said Sarah. “Just say the word and I will let up.”

I gritted my teeth. No way was I going to bow down to this

woman. Or agree with her stupid ideology. My anger sent a renewed sense of power through me, allowing met to push myself up again inch by inch.

“What?” said Sarah. She sounded panicked now. “How are you doing this? You shouldn't be able to fight back. You should be down.”

“Maybe … I'm not as weak as you think,” I said. Even just saying those words was pure agony, but I was not going to let her keep me down, not anymore.

I felt the pressure of the sounds increase, but I ignored it. I just forced myself up bit by bit, pushing back against the pressure, until I was now looking up at Sarah again.

She looked as stunned as if I had just punched her in the face. It was clear that she hadn't expected me to push back against her at all. And it was hard to do, but I wasn't about to let her break me, no matter how much pain she inflicted on me.

“Stop it,” said Sarah. She pointed at me in anger. “Get back down. Stop fighting back.”

I shook my head. “No. Why don't *you* just leave me *alone*?”

I shouted that word so loudly that it was like a bomb going off. Suddenly, Sarah staggered backwards, covering her ears in pain. And just as suddenly, the screaming and crashing sounds in my head went silent, which felt like pure bliss after suffering from them even for the brief period that I did.

Standing upright, I walked over to Sarah, who was now whimpering like a baby on the ground. Even though she was apparently just a hologram, I had somehow managed to hurt her, though she seemed more stunned at my resistance than anything.

“All right, Sarah,” I said, putting my hands on my waist as I looked down at her. "Tell me how to get out of here. Or else."

"Never," Sarah whimpered, still clutching her ears. "Why are you so mean? You're not supposed to hit back."

I rolled my eyes. "Sorry, but just because you're a girl doesn't mean I have to treat you nicely. I liked how you talked big, though, when you were dominating me earlier."

Sarah suddenly glared at me with her small, shifty eyes. "Then if you won't join us … we will kill you!"

Without warning, Sarah vanished before me. I stepped backwards, thinking this was some kind of attack, but then the lights suddenly turned on and I got to see where I was.

I was standing in the middle of a large, concrete room that looked like a training area of sorts, though it didn't look like the Training Room that the Young Neos had shown me before. Tall concrete pillars rose all around me, though they looked cracked and old from use.

Then I noticed something above. On the wall opposite me was a glass window that seemed to be the viewing area for people watching the fight. Beyond the window, I saw all five of the Young Neos, including Sarah herself, standing there like they had been watching me the whole time.

A crackling of a speaker echoed through the room and in the next second I heard Incantation's voice coming from the speaker above the window. "Kevin, we thought we could make you one of us, but it is obvious that we can't. Hopper, execute him."

Hopper nodded and raised a hand. I didn't know what he was going to do until suddenly, without warning, a portal appeared in the center of the room, hundreds of feet away from me.

But unlike the other portals Hopper had summoned, this one

had nothing but darkness beyond it. I felt a sucking sensation trying to drag me toward it, like a huge vacuum cleaner.

And that was when I realized how they were trying to kill me: They were trying to suck me into who-knows-where, just as Hopper had told me he could do with his powers what seemed like an eternity ago. And I saw no way for me to escape the room.

CHAPTER THIRTEEN

THE SUCKING FORCE OF the portal dragged me toward it. I turned and ran, but I could barely find traction on the floor. The portal's sucking power was too strong, like I was a piece of metal and it was a giant magnet.

I grabbed one of the nearest concrete pillars, digging my fingers deep into its surface with my super strength. While that kept me from being sucked into it, that didn't make the portal itself go away. I could feel its sucking power growing stronger and stronger as it attempted to devour me. I knew that eventually it would grow too powerful for me to escape, so I had to look for a way out fast.

I looked frantically around for an exit, but as far as I could tell the room was sealed off. That made me wonder how I got in here at all, but it didn't matter if there were even a hundred doors, because the portal's sucking power meant that if I let go of the concrete pillar, I'd just end up getting sucked into whatever void it was trying to draw me into.

I looked up at the Young Neos behind the glass above. They all looked satisfied to see me being drawn into their portal. Sarah, in particular, looked like she was watching a great movie and couldn't wait to see how it ended. I thought about screaming at them to stop, to let me go in peace, but that was only for a moment. These freaks wanted me dead and they were going to try their hardest to make sure that I didn't survive no matter how much I begged and pleaded for them to spare me.

It didn't help that the portal was sucking more than just me. The air was getting thinner because the portal was sucking the air into it, which made it harder to breathe in here. My grip on the pillar was getting weaker and weaker. Soon my grip would break completely and I would go flying into the portal.

But I had to escape. And if there wasn't a door, then I would just make one myself.

So I let go of the concrete pillar, but at the same time, I activated my super speed. I intended to outrun the portal's sucking force, going as fast as I could. I didn't know if it was possible to outrun it even with my super speed, but I had to give it a shot.

Immediately, I started running in the opposite direction of the portal. I made good distance, but the portal started sucking me in even harder than before. It was like it was a living thing, trying to keep me from escaping its hungry grasp, though I figured that was just Hopper increasing the power and strength of the portal.

I increased my speed and soon found myself getting farther and farther from the portal, inch by agonizing inch. I was now running so fast that I couldn't hear or see anything except for the breath of my lungs and the sucking sound of the portal behind me, which was having less and less power over me the farther away I got from it.

Then I sent a huge burst of speed through my legs and

launched through the air, moving so fast that I had no idea where I was going. All I knew was that I activated my super strength and smashed through a thick wall, rolling in the air before I landed on my back on the floor.

The impact jarred my senses, but only for a moment. In the next, I was sitting up, rubbing the back of my head. I looked up and saw that I was in the hallway of the House. There was a large hole in the wall above where I had broken out, but I could no longer feel the sucking force of the portal.

Rising to my feet, I knew I had to get out of here. I had to get home and tell Dad or Mom or someone what I learned. There was something very strange going on in this place and I was in no mood to figure it out on my own.

But before I could go anywhere, Ghost shot through the wall above me and, pointing at me, shouted, “Found him!”

Ghost fell toward me, forcing me to jump backwards to avoid him. He phased through the floor and, in a second, shot out of it again, his hands reaching toward me.

Instinctively I punched him, but my fist just went through his ghostly form without even touching him. I stepped backwards, while Ghost smirked at me.

“Forgot why I'm called 'Ghost,' huh?” said Ghost. “Here, let me give you a reminder.”

Ghost shot through me, his form passing through my body. Immediately, my bones became cold, so cold I screamed and fell to the floor as Ghost passed through the other side. He flew around me until he was facing me again, his arms folded across his chest and an annoying smirk on his face.

“How did that feel?” said Ghost. “Cold? I hope so. Because

that's another one of my powers; the ability to paralyze whoever I pass through."

I just grunted. My limbs felt like rocks. But I could still feel some movement in them, so I took a deep breath and activated my super speed, hoping that it would help me regain the feeling in my legs.

"But I am done talking," said Ghost. He raised his hands, like he was about to dive into me again. "One more time and you will never awaken again."

Just before Ghost could do that, however, another portal exploded into existence to my right. I immediately slammed my hands into the floor, using the metal plating to keep me from being sucked into the portal, but Ghost was not so lucky. He tried to fly away, but he was sucked into the portal, which immediately closed shut as soon as he passed through it.

I heard cursing above and looked up to see Hopper standing in the hole I had created. He looked horrified at what he'd done, holding his hands out with a terrified look on his face.

"Ghost!" Hopper shouted. "I didn't mean to do that. I—"

I slammed my fist into the wall, causing it to shake so hard that Hopper fell over backwards back into the room I had escaped from. I heard him scream as he fell, but I didn't stop long enough to hear him hit the floor.

Instead, I ran down the hall, although without my super speed, because I wasn't good at running fast indoors yet without slamming into walls. Besides, my current outfit wasn't fit for prolonged usage of super speed, which made me wish that Dad hadn't taken away my super suit.

As I turned down the hall, panels on both sides shifted to the side and twin laser cannons appeared. They immediately locked onto me and fired, but I dodged both laser blasts with quick applications of my super speed. But they kept shooting at me, so I flew through the air, still dodging their attacks, until I was right in the middle of them. The lasers aimed at me and fired, but at the last second I dropped, allowing the lasers to pass me and strike both cannons, causing them to explode.

I hit the floor with a roll and kept running. I had no idea where I was going. My only destination was 'anywhere but here.' It occurred to me that I was on Hero Island, which meant that I was near the NHA's base. Did the NHA even know about what the Young Neos were doing? If not, I'd be sure to let them know once I escaped.

But no sooner did that thought pass through my mind than the wall to my left exploded. I fell to the floor, covering my head as wiring and chunks of metal flew over me. Some of it hit me anyway, but I managed to avoid the bulk of it and looked up to see what had done that.

A large robot stood in the hole of the wall, aiming a massive cannon at me. But then I looked closer and realized that it wasn't actually a robot, but a humanoid mecha, because I saw Technical—wearing a mask that reminded me of Dad's helmet—sitting in the pilot seat in the center.

“What?” I said in disbelief. “Come on, now. How come *you* guys get awesome mechas and I don't?”

“Like it?” said Technical, who sounded crazy. “I made this on my own, though I was inspired by your dad's blueprints for a similar mecha. Not that it matters, really, because it is strong enough to break every bone in your body.”

I scrambled to my feet, but before I could do anything, a chain shot out of the mecha's cannon and wrapped around my body. It tightened, making me gasp for air, before it lifted me off the ground and threw me at the opposite wall.

I crashed into the wall hard and fell to the floor, stunned by the impact. I thought I felt a broken bone, but I wasn't sure. All I knew was that the mecha was now pulling me toward it while Technical laughed maniacally, like she was having a great time.

But I recovered when I was about halfway there and, activating my super strength, snapped the chain. Rolling to my feet, I grabbed the chain and, getting a firm grip on it, yanked it as hard as I could.

The mecha's arm ripped off with a loud tearing noise. Technical's maniacal laughing quickly turned into horrified shrieking, especially when the mecha fell over onto the floor. But just as it fell, the cockpit shot off and flew toward me, looking like a flying pod. Two laser guns appeared at its sides and started shooting at me. I dodged most of them, but one of them grazed my arm.

Instead of running, however, I sped toward the pod and, jumping into the air, landed on top of it. Technical looked up at me in shock, but then I smashed my fist through the glass and ripped her out of her seat.

Without Technical piloting it, the pod immediately fell, but not before I jumped off with Technical in my arms. The pod crashed into the floor and skidded and rolled until it crashed into the wall, where its cockpit immediately shattered upon impact and its engine exploded.

But that didn't stop Technical. She grabbed at me with her

mechanical arm, but I broke it with a single blow and dropped her to the floor. Technical landed on her back, but before she could get back up, I tied her up with the chains from her own mecha, wrapping her up so much that she couldn't even move.

"Hey!" Technical shouted, struggling against her chains. "Let me go, you bigot!"

I didn't even respond. I just shook my head and continued running down the hallway. My body was in pain from being slammed against the wall like that and I was pretty sure that something was broken, but I didn't stop to examine my injuries. I knew that I had to get out of here. I didn't have the luxury of lying around and healing.

I ran down yet another corridor, thinking as I ran. Let's see … I had already dealt with Ghost, Hopper, and Technical. That left only Incantation and Sarah, but I hadn't seen either of them since I escaped that room. Knowing Sarah, she had probably been traumatized by my refusal to bow down to her twisted ideology, while Incantation was probably trying to comfort her. That thought brought a smile to my face, but a weak one, because I was starting to get tired and all I wanted to do was rest.

At the end of the hall I came across two closed doors, which I figured had to lead somewhere important, so I punched my way through them, knocking them off their hinges. I dashed through the doors, but came to a stop when I saw where I was.

I had entered the antechamber of the House, or at least that was what it looked like. On either side of the room stood tall statues depicting legendary heroes like Omega Man and Lady Amazon while at the end was yet another set of doors that probably led outside. I was surprised that I had managed to find my way to the exit, but I didn't question my luck.

I just ran toward the door, but before I could get very far, a shadow passed over me and Incantation landed on the floor in front of me. She was carrying her wand, which was glowing with a deadly red glow, its light reflected in her eyes, making her look almost evil.

I stopped when I saw her and said, “Incantation, what are you doing? Get out of my way.”

Incantation shook her head. “No. You can't be allowed to leave, at least not until you're dead or converted to Vision.”

“The what?” I said. I shook my head. “It doesn't matter. I don't want to hurt you, but if that's what I need to do to get out of there, then so be it.”

But even as I said that, Incantation waved her wand and a sword appeared out of nowhere and flew toward me. I barely managed to dodge it in the nick of time, but then it curved through the air and flew toward me again.

This time, I dodged it, but grabbed its handle as it passed and snapped the blade in two over my knees before tossing it to the ground. I looked at Incantation, who was staring at me in shock.

“I don't have any patience for your magic tricks,” I said. “Either let me go or I won't be so nice anymore.”

“You keep saying that, but I don't think you actually want to harm me,” said Incantation. “Too bad *I* want to harm *you.*”

Incantation suddenly pulled out a long chain of metal rings from her cloak and hurled them at me. I dodged most of them, but a few cut my arms or shoulder, actually drawing blood. I gritted my teeth and covered the wounds, but I had no time to deal with them at the moment.

So I ran at Incantation, intending to knock her down with one blow. But before I could hit her, she twirled around and vanished in an instant, forcing me to come to a stop where she had been and look around. I didn't see her until I heard a sound above me and, looking up, saw Incantation standing on top of the fist of the Omega Man statue.

Before I could fly up after her, Incantation took off her hat and pointed its interior at me. A gigantic dove, of all things, flew out of the hat toward me, flapping its large wings as it soared toward me like a missile.

But I didn't hesitate. I pulled my fist back and, at the last second, punched the damn dove in the face. Immediately, the bird exploded into dozens of smaller doves, which flew away.

Surprised, I stood there for a moment before I suddenly heard Incantation behind me shout, "Got you!"

I turned around just in time to see a long ribbon flying at me. But I flew into the air, narrowly avoiding it, as it wrapped around the leg of the Omega Man statue. Looking down, I saw Incantation looking up at me in surprise and seemed too surprised to react.

I shot toward her. She raised her wand, aiming it at me, but I snatched her wand from her hand and snapped it as easily as if it was a stick. Then I landed behind her and twisted her arm behind her back, causing her to cry out in pain and let go of her ribbon rope.

"All right," I said in her ear, putting as much pressure on her arm as I could without actually breaking it. "I figure that without your little wand, you're completely powerless. So unless you want to spend the next few weeks with your arm in a cast, I suggest you give up and let me go."

I expected Incantation to agree with my demands, but then she suddenly said, "When did I *ever* say that I needed my wand to use my powers?"

I noticed Incantation's hands glowing. Then I heard a *clunk* behind me and looked over my shoulder just in time to see a huge wooden box falling toward me.

At the same time, Incantation brought her foot down on mine, making me gasp in pain and let her go. She vanished in front of me just as the box closed around my body, leaving only my head exposed.

"Hey!" I shouted, struggling against the box. "That was a dirty trick! Let me go!"

Although the box appeared to be made entirely of wood, even my super strength was no match for it. Maybe it was magically reinforced wood or maybe it was only made out of a substance that looked like wood but was something else entirely. Whatever the case, all I knew was that I didn't like it and it was uncomfortable.

Incantation appeared in front of me again, only this time she was carrying a very long, very sharp-looking sword that made me feel even more uncomfortable than before. "Don't you remember what I said when we first met, Bolt? No one can escape my magic boxes unless I want them to. So you're just going to stay right where I want you until I'm done with you."

I stopped struggling because I knew that she was telling the truth. I looked at the sword she carried. "Um, what are you going to do with that sword?"

Incantation smiled a very crazy, psychotic smile. "I'm going to perform my favorite magic trick on you: Poking swords through your body at different angles."

I gulped and realized that the box had holes in it that were the exact shape and size for her sword. "But you're not actually going to stab through me, right? It's just a trick."

"Nope," said Incantation. "I'm going to stab swords—and they're very sharp, too, I should know because I sharpened them myself—through every inch of your body. You won't die right away, but you will probably be screaming for mercy, mercy I won't grant you."

"Please," I said. "Don't do this. You're not in your right mind."

"On the contrary, I am perfectly sane," said Incantation. She pulled back her sword. "Too bad I can't say the same about you."

Incantation sent her sword aiming for the box. I renewed my struggle for freedom, but it was impossible. I could only watch as Incantation's sword shot toward me, wondering what it would feel like to be stabbed in the chest by a sword.

But then, out of nowhere, a hand grabbed Incantation's wrist, stopping her sword mere inches from the surface of the box. Both Incantation and I looked over at who had stopped her.

Standing right next to us was a middle-aged man in magician's robes … Thaumaturge, Incantation's master and one of the current leaders of the NHA.

CHAPTER FOURTEEN

I HAD NEVER SEEN Thaumaturge in person before, but I had seen a lot of pictures online. The man looked like a mixture between Doctor Strange and Gandalf. He wore a tall, battered magician's hat, the tip of which drooped slightly, while a short gray goatee hung off his chin. He was older, taller, and stronger than Incantation. His gray eyes were hard to read, but Thaumaturge had a reputation as mysterious, so that was no surprise. I was just glad that he had saved me.

"What?" said Incantation. She sounded terrified, much to my satisfaction. "Master, what are you doing here?"

"Reeve informed me that there was an intruder on Hero Island," said Thaumaturge. His voice was quiet, but impossible to ignore. "I came to see who it was." He glanced at me. "Who is this young man?"

"Bolt," said Incantation, though she still sounded afraid. "He's not in costume, but that's him."

"Genius's son?" said Thaumaturge. He looked at me more closely. "I did not believe I would ever get the privilege of meeting the son of one of my old colleagues. Tell me, how is

Genius doing nowadays?"

I relaxed, happy that Thaumaturge had come to my rescue. "Fine. He's been doing all right."

"Good to hear," said Thaumaturge. "I was worried about him when I heard that Master Chaos escaped, but I'm glad that he has managed to have a good life."

Then Thaumaturge looked at Incantation again. "Why are you trying to kill Genius's son?"

"Because he's against the Vision," said Incantation. "He beat us all and was just about to escape and tell the world about us."

I expected Thaumaturge to berate her for saying something so stupid, but to my horror, he merely stroked his chin and said, "Is that so? Is the Visionary aware of him?"

"No," said Incantation, shaking her head. "He gave us orders to kidnap Bolt, but he doesn't know what's happening here. Sarah said she was going to contact him, though."

"I see," said Thaumaturge. "Yes, he does need to know about this.

"What?" I said, drawing both Thaumaturge and Incantation's attention to me. "Thaumaturge, what are you talking about? She was trying to *kill* me."

"I know that," said Thaumaturge. "But I also know that the Visionary gave us permission to eliminate anyone who tried to expose our existence to the world. And I have never been one to question the Visionary's orders."

"What the hell?" I said. "You're on their side, too? Who is the Visionary?"

"I'm not going to divulge that secret to you," said Thaumaturge. "Suffice to say, however, that you are clearly incapable of understanding the Vision. It is sad, because as Genius's son I thought you'd be smarter than most, but I see that I was mistaken."

I had wondered how the Young Neos had been getting away with kidnapping and torturing me, how they had been getting away with their insane ideology and cult-like nature. I had thought they were keeping their true nature a secret from the NHA, but now I understood the truth: Thaumaturge was on their side and hiding their true nature from the rest of the NHA.

"It is pretty obvious, then, what we must do," said Thaumaturge. He took his hand off Incantation's wrist. "Finish him off."

"Wait!" I shouted. "If you kill me, my dad will get suspicious. So will lots of other people. They'll expose your little conspiracy before you succeed in whatever you're trying to do."

Thaumaturge looked at me in confusion. "*Before* we succeed? I don't think you understand, Bolt. We have *already* succeeded."

"And your death won't incriminate us," said Incantation. She pulled her sword back again. "We've erased deaths from the public before. We can easily do it again."

Just as Incantation was about to stab me, something smashed through the windows of the entry hall. Both Thaumaturge and Incantation looked up just in time to see a large white drone—which I immediately recognized as Seeker One—soar into the room. It aimed one of its guns at them, causing Thaumaturge and Incantation to aim their glowing hands at it.

But Seeker One was faster. It fired a beam of energy, but not at Thaumaturge or Incantation. The energy beam struck the floor a few feet from them and there was a bright flash of light that forced the two magicians to cover their eyes. When the light faded, however, I was surprised at who was standing there.

Dad—in his full Genius costume—stood in front of Thaumaturge and Incantation. His gauntlets were sparking with electricity and, although I couldn't see his face, I could tell that he was very, very angry.

"Genius?" said Thaumaturge, looking at Dad in astonishment. "What are *you* doing here?"

"Saving my son," Dad replied, his voice slightly muffled through his helmet.

Incantation snarled. "You might have technology, but it's no match for our magic!"

Incantation threw her sword at Dad, but Dad turned the dial on his belt and disappeared. Incantation and Thaumaturge looked around wildly, trying to find Dad, but then he reappeared behind them and grabbed their shoulders with his sparkling hands.

Immediately, Incantation and Thaumaturge screamed as the electricity from Dad's gauntlets flowed through their bodies. Dad didn't even flinch. He just stood there silently, charging electricity through them, until both Incantation and Thaumaturge collapsed onto the floor. The only way I knew they were both still alive was how they twitched every now and then.

Lowering his hands, Dad turned to face me. "Are you okay?"

I hadn't realized it, but my mouth was hanging open. "Uh, yeah. But how did you know where I was?"

"Because I've had Valerie keeping track of you and she told me you were here," said Dad. He looked down at the unconscious Thaumaturge and Incantation at his feet. "I just wish that I hadn't had to meet my old friend again like this."

"Dad, do you know what's going on here?" I said. "Do you know what's up with Thaumaturge and the Young Neos?"

"I don't, but Triplet does," said Dad. His hands balled into fists. "But we can talk more about that once we're safe."

Dad raised his hand and shot a laser from his gauntlet at the box's hinges. The hinges snapped, allowing me to push open the door and step out of the cramped box.

"Come," said Dad. "We need to get out of here before the rest of the NHA arrives."

Dad put a hand on my shoulder and then twisted the Teleportation Buckle. In an instant, we left the House and were back in Dad's laboratory, which was built underneath our house back in Texas.

But we weren't alone. Triplet was leaning against the wall, his arms folded over his chest. Once he saw us, he pushed himself off the wall and stood up straight.

"Ted?" said Triplet. "How did it go?"

"As well as it could, under the circumstances," said Dad with a sigh. "But your theory turned out to be correct. Thaumaturge was compromised."

Triplet cursed in Japanese under his breath. "I knew *someone* in the upper ranks of the NHA was, but I didn't know it was Thaumaturge. It doesn't surprise me, though; he was always a freak."

"What's going on here?" I said, looking between Dad and Triplet in confusion. "What theory? What are you even talking about?"

"We're talking about my investigation," said Triplet. "Or rather, what I found through my investigation. And none of it is pretty."

"What did you find out?" I said. "Weren't you investigating whether Plutarch was planning to take over the United States?"

"I was," said Triplet, nodding. "But through the course of my investigation, I discovered something far worse than Plutarch."

"What would that be?" I said. "And what are you even doing back here in my house? I thought you were going somewhere else."

"Because your father here is one of the few people I trust enough not to sell me out to those who might want to kill me," said Triplet. "Trust me, what I know would get me killed if the wrong people knew about it."

I looked at Dad. "Does Mom know that Triplet is here?"

"She does," said Dad. "She isn't happy about it, as you can imagine, but she accepts his presence." He looked at Triplet. "Mieko, why don't you share your findings with Bolt? He deserves to know, given what he was just put through."

"All right," said Triplet. He looked around, like he thought someone might be eavesdropping on us, even though we were the only three people here in the Lab. "As you know, I was investigating Adam Plutarch, who I believed was running for President of the United States in order to turn the country into a dictatorship. My initial theory, which seemed borne out by the evidence I found, was that Plutarch had never truly reformed but was instead using the growing anti-neohero sentiment in the country to win the election."

"Right," I said, though I was really thinking about my conversation with Plutarch that seemed like a long time ago now. "Someone hired you to do that, right?"

"Yes," said Triplet. "A man who called himself the Citizen hired me to investigate Plutarch. But since our last talk, I made a deadly discovery that, if brought to the public's attention, could turn the entire election on its head and maybe even change the country as we know it."

"What is that discovery?" I said.

Triplet jammed his hands into the pockets of his overcoat. "I discovered that a cult called Vision has embedded itself in the Neohero Alliance. It is led by the Visionary, who I believe bailed out Steel Skin, Firespirit, and Nail Gun from Ultimate Max for the purpose of framing Plutarch."

"Who is the Visionary?" I said. "And how did you discover this conspiracy?"

"Not conspiracy," Triplet corrected me. "Well, I guess you could call it that, but it operates more like a cult. As for who the Visionary is, I don't know for sure yet, but I do know that he controls the entire group from the shadows, directing their movements and giving orders in order to achieve their plans."

"Thaumaturge mentioned someone named the Visionary," I said. "But I still don't understand how you found out about this."

"I probably wouldn't have if I hadn't gone to Plutarch's mansion after Nail Gun's attack," said Triplet. "I managed to search Nail Gun's body and stole his phone, which had a lot of emails and texts from this same Visionary I told you about. It's how I learned that someone in the NHA leadership was part of the cult and was ensuring that the organization was following the dictates of the Visionary even if no one realized it."

"Did you trace the texts and emails back to the Visionary's phone?" I said.

"No," said Triplet. "I tried, but the Visionary must change his email addresses and phone numbers regularly, because the email address and phone numbers I investigated were no longer in use. A smart way to avoid getting caught, that's for sure."

"You described Vision as a cult," I said. "What do you mean by that?"

"He means they act like one," said Dad, causing me to look at him. He had removed his helmet and was holding it under his arm, a frown on his face. "They brainwash younger neoheroes into their group, usually through the Neohero Academy on Hero Island. I believe that that is how the Young Neos, such as Incantation, were taken into it, because most of them were students at the Academy before they joined the team."

"Yes," said Triplet, nodding. "And they worship their leader like a god. They do not question him or his dictates. They believe wholeheartedly in their mission, which they refer to as the 'Vision.' They put on a kind, accepting face in public, but behind every face is a raging psychopath ready to kill anyone who opposes their grand Vision for society."

"They're brainwashing students through the Academy?" I said in shock. "Why don't we tell the NHA about this? Shouldn't they be aware of this cult and what it is doing?"

Dad and Triplet exchanged looks, like they knew something I didn't. I didn't understand it. Was I missing something?

Finally, Dad looked at me and said, "Because no one would believe us. You saw Thaumaturge. He is a part of the cult. It is possible, also, that some of the other NHA leaders are also cultists, but we don't know that for sure."

"But wouldn't they listen to you guys anyway?" I said. "I

mean, both of you were once members of the NHA. Dad, you were even one of the Four Founders. Don't you think they would at least hear you out, even if they didn't agree right away?"

"I doubt it," said Dad. "The rest of the NHA hasn't quite forgiven me for quitting the organization, even if they understand why."

"More than that, I already tried investigating a conspiracy within the NHA years ago," said Triplet. "I was kicked out when they found out what I was doing. They claimed that I was threatening the unity of the organization and that there was no conspiracy in the NHA at all."

I looked at Triplet in surprise. "You mean you didn't leave voluntarily?"

"Oh, I technically did, but I wouldn't have had to if the NHA hadn't attacked me and painted me like some kind of loon," said Triplet, shaking his head. "I didn't even get very far. I just started asking questions and noticing certain oddities, such as how many young neoheroes that came out of the Academy all shared essentially the same basic ideology and always reacted with great hostility if you ever questioned it. It wasn't even a serious investigation at the time, which is why I was so surprised when I faced the blow back that I did."

"Who led the charges against you?" I said.

"Thaumaturge, actually," said Triplet. He chuckled darkly. "Even before I started asking the wrong questions, Thaumaturge didn't like me, though I assumed that was because I asked too many questions about how his mystical powers worked. But apparently, he was the one behind it all."

"Thaumaturge is not just in charge of the Young Neos," Dad

said. “He is also the headmaster of the Academy. He is in charge of deciding what to teach the students there.”

“So are you saying that Thaumaturge has been brainwashing young neoheroes?” I said. “And no one has ever noticed this?”

“No one thought of it as brainwashing,” said Triplet. “All Thaumaturge ever said was that he taught his students how to be 'good' and 'responsible' superheroes. It was hard to prove that there was a problem because his students were always very good at pretending to be saner than they are.”

“And not all of the teachers or students succumbed to the brainwashing, either,” said Dad. “It was hard to prove that there was any brainwashing going on when most of the faculty said otherwise.”

“But now we know for sure,” said Triplet. He smiled. “Vindication is sweet.”

I looked at Dad again. “Is that why you didn't send me to the Academy for training? Because of Thaumaturge's teachings?”

Dad nodded. “Yes. I saw it as early as the very first class of the school, which Thaumaturge taught. At first I tried to ignore it, but I found myself growing disgusted with what I knew was going on in that school, even when no one else agreed with me and I could not prove that anything nefarious was going on. That was another reason I resigned; it was my way of protesting what I saw was being taught in the Academy, though based on what I've learned, my resignation did nothing to change what they taught to the students there.”

“Did you ever believe the charges laid out against Triplet?” I said to Dad.

“At first I did,” said Dad. He sounded ashamed. “But I was

always a little doubtful, because I knew Triplet was smart and what he was saying fit with what I knew. But it wasn't until he found Nail Gun's phone and showed me what was on it that I realized he was telling the truth."

"How long has Thaumaturge been part of Vision?" I said. "How long has this indoctrination been going on?"

"I don't know," said Triplet. "Like I said, Vision is very good at covering its tracks. My theory is that Thaumaturge was the first Vision agent to join the NHA, but it's possible he's converted others since. We know, at least, that he's converted the Young Neos, and probably other young neoheroes, too."

"But why?" I said. "What is the end game of Vision? What is the Visionary trying to do?"

"That's the question, isn't it?" said Triplet. "My theory is that the Visionary is trying to create an army of brainwashed neoheroes who will serve him without question and he is using the Vision ideology to accomplish that."

"World domination, then?" I said. "Like most supervillains?"

"That is very likely," said Dad. "An army of brainwashed neoheroes could make you the most powerful man on Earth. And what better way to create that army than through the Academy, a place where many impressionable young people with incredible powers go through?"

"Then we have to stop them," I said. "We need to expose their plans to the world."

"Nice idea, but unrealistic," said Triplet. "We lack any real proof to support our assertions. It will be our word against Thaumaturge's, and Thaumaturge is far more respected than us. Even Nail Gun's texts and emails aren't proof enough."

"No one in the media would ever listen to us anyway," said Dad in a disgruntled voice. "They're too obsessed with the election to care about what a conspiracy nut, a retired superhero long past his prime, and a young kid like yourself have to say about a cult operating within the NHA."

"Then what should we do?" I said. "Just let them get away with this?"

"No," said Triplet, shaking his head. "As it turns out, I also know what Vision's next move will be."

"Really?" I said. "How did you figure it out?"

"Nail Gun's phone," said Triplet. "I found an email from the Visionary stating that if Nail Gun failed to kill Plutarch yesterday, then he could try again at the first presidential debate between Sagan and Plutarch in Austin, which is on Monday."

"But Nail Gun is dead," I said. "That means he can't try to assassinate Plutarch again. Even if he wasn't, the debate will probably have a lot of extra security to make sure no one harms Plutarch or Sagan."

"You're assuming that that means that Vision has canceled the assassination," said Triplet. "It's possible, but unlikely. I think that they will go through with it anyway. They seem to hate Plutarch and want him dead, so I doubt they would let him stay alive until Election Day."

"What about Sagan?" I said. "Are they going to try to get him, too?"

"Possibly, but none of the texts or emails I read even mentioned him," said Triplet. "Vision might want him to win because he's more pro-neohero than Plutarch, which means he's less likely to support anti-neohero laws that would make it harder for Vision to operate. I doubt he's connected with the cult, because as far as I can tell Vision only recruits neoheroes and Sagan has no powers of his own."

"What are we going to do, then?" I said.

"Go to the debate and try to stop the assassination, assuming that they haven't canceled it," said Triplet. "With luck, we can at least catch Vision's assassin, who might be able to tell us more about the cult and its leader and his ultimate plans."

"I want to help," I said.

"Kevin—" said Dad in a warning voice, but I whirled around to face him before he could finish.

"Dad, I know what you're about to say, but you're wrong," I said. "I know it's dangerous, but at this point I can't just sit back and let you guys deal with it. I know too much. Besides, if catching Vision's assassin will keep other young neoheroes from becoming like the Young Neos, then I have to do it no matter what."

"Kid's got a point," said Triplet, nodding. "We have no idea what Vision will try at the debate, so we'll need all the help we can get."

Dad looked like he didn't approve of this at all, but then he sighed and said, "All right. But we'll need to be careful. Now that Vision knows that we're aware of them, they will try to kill us if we get in their way."

"Of course," I said. I looked at Triplet. "So how are we going to get into the debate without being seen?"

"I think I know how," said Triplet. "Listen closely, because we're going to need every bit of time we have if we're going to pull this plan off without any flaws."

CHAPTER FIFTEEN

ON THE NIGHT OF the first presidential debate of the election season, I sat in the audience, in the very back row, where I had a good view of the debate stage. There were a few hundred people sitting around me, chatting and talking as we waited for Plutarch and Sagan to come out on stage and start the debate. Dozens of cameras from all of the major news networks were near the debate stage, most of them not yet activated, while cameramen operating the cameras checked on their equipment to make sure it was working correctly.

Looking around, I didn't see anything suspicious. The people in the audience seemed like normal, non-powered individuals, as did the cameramen and other studio staff. I noticed security guards and Secret Service agents everywhere, but I didn't look at any of them for too long because I didn't want to arouse anyone's suspicion. I just wish I knew who the assassin was, but Triplet had already told me that the assassin was likely undercover, meaning that he could have been anyone in the audience or even among the Secret Service or security guards.

I probably shouldn't have been too worried, because no one

knew that I was actually Bolt. In fact, no one paid me any attention whatsoever, but I still rubbed my suit-up watch anyway, which Dad had returned to me yesterday so I could have access to my suit. I was happy to have it back, but that didn't stop me from wondering what I'd do if Vision's assassin came after me.

I took this moment to think over our plan, because the debate was going to start sometime within the next five minutes and I would probably not have a chance to think about it again soon.

The plan was pretty simple. Triplet and I would go to the debate so we could deal with the assassin in person, while Dad stayed home in the Lab to monitor communications coming in and out of the building in which the debate was taking place. The reason for that was because Triplet believed that the assassin might be in communication with the Visionary, so if the assassin attempted to contact the Visionary while in here, then Dad could hack into his communication line and use it to track down the Visionary himself.

Our goal was to stop the assassin before he laid even one finger on Plutarch. I was sitting here in the audience, just in case the assassin was among the people in attendance, while Triplet was somewhere backstage, sneaking around in case the assassin was among the studio staff. I wasn't sure how Triplet was avoiding detection backstage or how he had managed to get me a ticket to the debate, but I supposed he had his ways of doing things and I shouldn't worry about them too much.

Regardless, I still worried that something would go wrong. Vision had to know that we were going to try to stop them today; Thaumaturge and Incantation, at least, had to expect it. It was entirely possible that they had canceled the assassination of

Plutarch or pushed it back to a later date. Maybe nothing of importance was going to happen tonight and we'd just waste our time, but that seemed unlikely. According to Triplet, it was going to be harder and harder to assassinate Plutarch as Election Day drew closer, so if Vision wanted to kill Plutarch, now was the time.

Speaking of Plutarch, I had called him and told him about our findings. I had expected him to call off the debate, but Plutarch said he wasn't afraid of any assassins, because he had already been the target of multiple assassination attempts, both before and after his supervillain days, and he was not going to let yet another one keep him from debating Sagan. He even said he'd be the bait to lure out the assassin (and, by extension, Vision) so we could catch him, which seemed suicidally reckless to me, but Plutarch had insisted upon it. Considering how he had killed Nail Gun personally, he probably could take care of himself.

I raised my hand to my earcom and, activating it, whispered, “Dad, have you picked up any communications going out of the building?”

“Negative,” Dad's voice crackled over the earcom, but it was very quiet so that no one would hear it. “Lots of messages and phone calls being sent by the people in the audience to friends and family outside, but nothing regarding Vision or the assassin. I imagine the assassin is probably not going to be contacting the Visionary this late in the plan, but I'll continue to monitor all communications in and out of the building just the same.”

“Okay,” I said, glancing around the audience. “I still haven't seen any sign of the assassin, either. Triplet?”

“Same here,” came Triplet's voice. “I haven't seen anyone or anything very suspicious. It's very quiet backstage."

"Think the assassin bailed at the last minute?" I said.

"Possibly, but it is equally possible that we're dealing with a highly professional assassin who is waiting until the right moment to strike," said Triplet. "Probably a superhuman, I imagine, perhaps one with either mind powers or the ability to shape shift."

"Shape shift?" I said. I looked at my chair. "Are you telling me that I might be sitting on an assassin?"

"No, but he could be anyone," said Triplet. "Keep your eyes and ears open. Knowing how Vision operates, we can't afford to let our guard down for any reason. This may be our only chance to stop them, so don't screw it up."

I was about to say that of course I wasn't going to screw it up, but then I heard a tiny click, which meant that Triplet was done talking. Not that I needed to talk to him right now, of course, because the debate was about to start any second. The assassin was probably going to make his move once Plutarch and Sagan were out on stage.

A few minutes later, the moderator—a middle-aged guy whose name I didn't know—walked out onto the stage and announced to the people that Plutarch and Sagan were about to enter and start the debate. Excited murmurs went through the audience, but I took this moment to look for any suspicious behavior in the audience. As usual, I didn't see anything suspicious, so perhaps the assassin was still blending in with everyone else.

So I sat back and watched as the moderator called out Sagan and Plutarch's names. Sagan came out first, walking slowly onto stage and waving and smiling at the audience like a friendly old grandpa. Half of the audience cheered him, while the other half was silent but obviously annoyed, which helped me figure out who were the Sagan fans and who were the Plutarch fans. I caught a glimpse of Sagan's assistant, the telepath June, standing in the darkness behind the stage. She was watching the Senator walk over to his podium, but she stepped back out of view quickly. I had almost forgotten about her, but I couldn't get up and talk to her and find out if she had picked up thoughts from anyone that might lead to the assassin's identity.

A second later, Plutarch entered the stage. Unlike Sagan, Plutarch walked with his usual swagger and confidence. He waved at the people, a confident grin on his face, while his fans went crazy, chanting, "Plutarch! Plutarch! Plutarch!" over and over again. I noticed that most of Sagan's supporters were sneering at Plutarch, a few even shouting insults at him, but their insults were drowned out by the cheering and chants of his supporters. But none of Sagan's fans looked like they were about to pull out a gun and shoot Plutarch or anything. Now I was starting to think that maybe the assassin wasn't here at all or at least wasn't in the audience.

While the moderator opened the debate with an introduction to the audience about the topic of the debate (it was about the US government's relation with neoheroes), I looked around at the edges of the room. The security guards and Secret Service agents were still standing at their positions, hands on their weapons as they looked around for anyone who might try to harm Sagan or Plutarch. I wondered if those guys would be enough to stop the assassin, but if the assassin was a superhuman, as Triplet suspected, then they probably wouldn't be very effective at defending Plutarch and Sagan.

But that was why we were here. Assuming all went well, soon the entire world would know about Vision and its twisted goals. I felt angry whenever I thought about how Vision had corrupted the Young Neos and other young superheroes, but I still stayed in my seat because there was no reason for me to get up and do anything just yet.

Then, all of a sudden, my earcom crackled and Triplet's voice said, "Bolt, there's someone backstage here."

Glancing at the people around me to make sure no one was paying attention to me (they weren't; all eyes were on Plutarch and Sagan), I put my ear to my earcom and muttered, "Who is it?"

"Not sure," said Triplet. "But—"

Triplet's voice immediately went silent. I tapped my earcom again, saying, "Triplet? Triplet, are you there? Hello? Hello?"

No answer. Just ominous silence.

I tapped my earcom again, but this time said, "Dad, I just lost Triplet. Can you hear me?"

"Yes, but barely," said Dad. His voice sounded distorted in my ear. "Triplet's earcom has disappeared from the radar. Did he remove it?"

"I don't know," I said. "He just said he saw someone backstage, but didn't get a chance to tell me who it was."

"That's not good," said Dad. "Listen, you should stay in your seat while I try to reconnect with Triplet's earcom. If that assassin is nearby, he's probably going to try to attack any minute now. You need to be there so you can stop him."

I nodded and said, "Sure. I'll call you again if something else happens."

"Affirmative," said Dad. "Stay safe."

My earcom clicked off again, but even though I told Dad I was just going to sit here, I wanted to get up and go look for Triplet. I didn't know if Triplet was dead or harmed or what, and I didn't like not knowing that, either. Yet Dad had a point that I couldn't leave, because if I did, the assassin might attack and I wouldn't be able to protect Plutarch or stop the assassin.

So I looked back down at the debate stage where Sagan and Plutarch were already in the middle of the debate itself. It was Plutarch's turn to speak now, and as usual, his voice was booming and clear.

"Hey, I like neoheroes," Plutarch said, his smile wide, if a bit fake-looking, "but I also think that they should be held responsible for the destruction they cause every time they fight with other freaky losers in tights. What's so wrong about that? Nothing. It's just common sense."

Plutarch seemed to be rambling, so I expected to see Sagan roll his eyes, but instead, the Senator was staring at Plutarch with surprising intensity. Maybe Sagan was just listening so he could come up with a good response to Plutarch's point, but I doubted it, because he looked like he was focusing on something else.

Then I noticed movement in the shadows backstage, from where Sagan and Plutarch had entered. In the next instant, something small and round flew out of the entrance. It looked like a gray metal ball, which clanked on the floor right in between Sagan and Plutarch's podiums. It landed on the floor with a loud *clank*, drawing the attention of both Sagan and Plutarch to it. And unless my eyes were playing tricks on me, Sagan didn't look surprised when he saw it.

A split second later, the ball exploded, creating a thick smoke cloud that immediately covered the entire room. People in the audience screamed and shouted while the Secret Service and security guards started shouting and running around, though it sounded like most of them were just as incapacitated as the people were. I looked around, but couldn't see anything with all of this smoke, especially when the people in the audience started getting up from their seats and fleeing for the nearest exits. The woman sitting next to me accidentally hit me in the face with her purse as she and her husband crawled over the seats in an attempt to get away, coughing loudly the whole time.

But I didn't move from my seat. Noticing that everyone was distracted by the bomb and the thick smoke, I dropped down to the floor of my seat and activated my suit-up watch. In an instant, I was suited up in my costume without being seen by the fleeing and screaming people. So I stood up, but the smoke was just too thick to see through. My goggles protected my eyes, but when I inhaled the smoke, I coughed and hacked for a moment, which made my eyes water.

Then I heard gun shots go off, along with more screams from the people in the audience. It sounded like a gun had been fired on the debate floor, so I flew through the smoke and landed on the debate stage, but it was still too thick for me to see, so I spun my arms around as fast as I could, generating enough wind to blow away a good chunk of the smoke, which revealed a startling sight to me:

Adam Plutarch lay slumped against his podium, his right shoulder bloody, while Barnabas Sagan was nowhere to be seen.

CHAPTER SIXTEEN

I RAN UP TO Plutarch's podium and, shaking his shoulder, said, "Mr. Plutarch, are you okay? Can you hear me? Are you still conscious?"

To my relief, Plutarch's eyes flickered open and he looked up at me, but he no longer looked as confident as he did before. He looked weak and almost dead, which was no surprise, given his age and injuries.

"Kid …" Plutarch coughed. "Ow …"

"Who shot you, Mr. Plutarch?" I said. "Can you remember? Or at least tell me where your assassin fled?"

Plutarch just pointed a weak finger at the entrance to the backstage.

"That's where the assassin went?" I said.

Plutarch nodded weakly. "Y-Yeah …"

Then he slid off the podium, but I caught him and gently lowered him to the debate floor. Once I was sure he was safe, I stood up and ran off to the backstage, using my super speed to give me a boost.

Backstage, the air was much clearer due to the lack of smoke, but it was in chaos. Interns and assistants and other members of the studio staff were either running around in fear or hiding under tables or behind other furniture, like they thought someone might try to kill them. I stopped when I saw the confusion, because I couldn't see where the assassin had fled, or who the assassin even was for that matter.

Then I noticed a young woman, probably only a couple years older than me, lying with a bad bruise on her forehead in front of the curtains. Her glasses were askew and cracked, but she still appeared to be alive, so I knelt down next to her and, shaking her shoulder, said, “Hey, are you all right? Hello?”

The intern shook her head and looked at me. She seemed dazed, like she was waking from a dream. “Huh? What? Who are you?”

“Bolt,” I said. “Can you tell me who did this to you?”

The intern blinked and then groaned, grabbing the bruise on her head. “Oh … I think it was that tall blonde lady, June or whatever. Sagan's assistant.”

“Why did she hit you?” I said.

“I don't know,” said the intern. “I just remember the smoke bomb going off and everyone going crazy. Then I heard a gun shot and I went to go see what was going on, but then June and Sagan appeared and June hit me with a pipe, said something about getting Sagan to safety or something.”

“Where did June and Sagan go?” I said.

The intern pointed further to the back. “I don't know for sure, but it looked like they were going that way before June knocked me out.”

“Thanks,” I said.

I stood up and ran toward the exit. As I made my way through the backstage chaos, I realized that June was the assassin all along. And not only was she the assassin, she was also obviously kidnapping Sagan, using the chaos created by the smoke bomb to get him out of here before anyone could stop her. It made me wonder what Vision wanted with Sagan, but I wasn't going to ponder that. I just needed to stop June before she took the Senator to wherever she planned to take him.

Bursting through the back exit, I saw June getting Sagan into the back of a limousine. She closed the door behind him as soon as he got in and then jumped into the driver's seat, at which point the limo's engine roared to life and the vehicle started to move.

I wasn't about to let her escape, however. I soared through the air, easily overtaking the vehicle, and landed directly in front of it. I saw June's startled expression through the windshield, but instead of stopping the car, she increased the speed.

I jerked out my arms and caught the limo just as it rammed into me. I skidded backwards a few inches, but I held my ground, using my super strength to prevent the limo from going any further. The wheels were starting to screech against the pavement as June increased the vehicle's speed, but I didn't budge at all.

Instead, I took one hand off the front of the vehicle and then smashed my fist straight down through the hood, smashing apart the engine. The car immediately died, its tires ceasing to screech against the pavement.

But just as I stepped away from the car, the driver's door opened and June stepped out. I expected her to hit me with some kind of mental attack, but instead she pulled out a gun and started shooting at me. I dodged the bullets easily, however, and then zoomed over to her and knocked the gun out of her hand before she even knew what I was doing.

Then, still moving fast, I grabbed her arm and twisted it behind her back. June yelled in pain before I hit her on the head, instantly knocking her out. She collapsed into my arms before I lowered her onto the ground. There was a bad bruise on her head where I hit her, but she seemed to be alive, which was good, because we needed her to be alive so we could interrogate her later.

Then I remembered that Sagan was still in the car, so I ran over to the back passenger's side and ripped open the door. To my relief, Sagan was sitting unharmed in the back, with a seat belt on and everything, though he looked shaken and worried.

"Senator, are you okay?" I said. "Did June hurt you?"

Sagan shook his head. "N-No, young man, she did not. But what happened? I remember smoke and gun shots, but it all happened so fast that it feels like a dream."

I ripped off Sagan's seat belt and helped him out of the car as I said, "You were almost kidnapped, Senator, by your own assistant. June also tried to assassinate Mr. Plutarch in order to distract the Secret Service from your kidnapping."

"What?" said Sagan. He looked at June, who lay unconscious on the ground where I had left her. "Oh my god. Why would June do such a thing? I thought she was loyal to me."

"I don't know her exact motives, but I suspect that she's working for a dangerous cult called Vision," I said. "They hired her to assassinate Plutarch and kidnap you. And she would have gotten away with it, too, if I hadn't been here tonight."

"Vision, hmm?" said Sagan. He was recovering rather quickly

from his shock, but maybe the old man was tougher than he looked. “Where did you learn about them?”

I frowned, wondering why Sagan seemed so interested. “From a friend who has been investigating them. Why do you ask?”

“Oh, no reason,” said Sagan with a shrug. He looked at the unconscious June mournfully. “But I am thankful that you saved me. I thought that my loyal assistant was merely trying to get me to safety, but I guess she was really trying to take me away somewhere no one else could find me. That would have ruined my chances at winning the presidency for sure.”

“I know,” I said. “Now please come with me, Senator. We need to get you back into the building and let the Secret Service know that you're safe.”

Sagan nodded, but then, all of a sudden, I heard a chipper ring tone come from the right pocket of his pants. Sagan quickly slipped his hand into the pocket as the ring tone continued playing, though it sounded muffle due to being in his pocket.

“What's that noise?” I said.

“Oh, it is just my phone,” said Sagan as he drew his smartphone out of his pocket with shaking hands. “I wonder who —Oh!”

Sagan accidentally dropped his phone onto the pavement onto its screen. Sagan started to bend over to pick it up, but I said, “Don't worry, Senator. I'll get it for you.”

Before Sagan could say anything, I bent over, picked up his phone, and was just about to hand it over to him when I noticed who was calling. It showed a picture of a familiar-looking smiling teenage girl with short, green hair. Underneath the picture and its number was a single word: 'Sarah.'

I looked up at Sagan. “Senator, who is Sarah?”

Sagan didn't meet my gaze. His eyes darted from side to side, like he was looking for an escape route, as he said, “My granddaughter, obviously. Why do you ask?”

I looked at the image of Sarah on his phone again. “Senator … your granddaughter wouldn't happen to be named Sarah Jane Watson, would she?”

Without warning, I heard crashing and screaming sounds in my head. I yelled in pain and staggered backwards, dropping Sagan's phone onto the pavement again. I fell down to my knees, grabbing my head with my hands, trying to make the pain go away, but there was nothing I could do about it.

Then Sagan grabbed my chin and forced me to look up at his face. He no longer looked like the kindly old man I'd known before. Instead, he looked like he was consumed with rage, his eyes popping out behind his glasses and his mouth twisted in an angry scowl.

“S-Senator …” I said, but the screaming and crashing sounds in my head made it almost impossible for me to hear myself. “What …”

“Don't call me 'Senator,' boy,” said Sagan. The kindness in his voice had vanished, replaced by a cold hatred that shocked me. “I never liked that title anyway. So plain. So ordinary. Not fitting for a man of my vision.”

I gasped. “Are you … Visionary?”

Sagan nodded. “Correct, boy. And you are Kevin Jason, son of Theodore Jason, also known as Genius, the famous, retired superhero and one of the Four Founders of the Neohero Alliance.”

"How did you know that?" I said in shock. "I've never told you my secret identity."

Sagan tapped the side of his head with his finger. "Your mind is an open book to me, boy. I know your every secret, your every desire. I know you and your little detective friend were here to stop me. Too bad you were too late."

I tried to stand and fight, but the screaming and crashing sounds in my head practically paralyzed me. "But … June …"

Sagan chuckled. "June? She never had any powers. She was just an ordinary woman, always was and always will be. I only told everyone that she was a telepath so they would not suspect me of having powers. And it worked very well, considering how not even the G-Men have ever suspected me of being a superhuman."

Then Sagan removed his hand from my chin. "But I'm not going to stand here and reveal all my plans and secrets to you and give you a chance to beat me. IBut neither am I going to let you live knowing my identity, not after I spent so many, many years keeping it a secret from the public."

Suddenly, the pressure in my head increased. I cried out in pain, grabbing my head with my hands, but the pain just got worse and worse. It felt like my head was being squeezed between a huge metal clamp and getting tighter by the second.

"I could just erase your memories of me, as Sarah and I did to Steel Skin and Firespirit when they were caught so no one would know that I had hired them," said Sagan, his voice sounding far away even though he stood just a few feet in front of me. "But you know too much, even if I erased my identity from you. I will just turn you into a vegetable. No one will ever know, because I will tell everyone that June, using her mental powers, did it in order to protect my life from your murderous rampage. And everyone will believe me, because everyone *always* believes me."

I could feel my mind being picked apart bit by bit. I tried to fight against it, but I couldn't. I didn't have any mental powers of my own. I was completely defenseless against Sagan's assault.

I heard my earcom crackle in my ear and then Dad's worried, frantic voice. "Kevin! What's the problem? I just saw on the news that Plutarch was shot at the debate! Are you and Triplet all right? Hello?"

I couldn't answer. It was becoming harder and harder to concentrate. Sagan's mental powers kept hammering away at my mind. Even thinking was becoming a chore. It was almost worse than being stabbed by Nail Gun.

I looked up at Sagan. He was staring down at me with cold eyes. It was like staring into the eyes of a snake. I tried to reach up to him to stop him, but he easily slapped away my hand like it was nothing.

"You have a strong will," said Sagan. "But I have broken much stronger wills in the past. Sooner or later, everyone breaks. And I will shatter you."

Thinking … becoming … impossible. I just wanted to lie down and get it over with. I almost stopped fighting, because I figured that it would be easier and much less painful to let him win than to fight a losing battle.

But then I remembered what Triplet had said, about how Vision had brainwashed so many young neoheroes over the years. I remembered what would happen if I failed, how such a terrible villain would continue his reign of terror and might even become the President of the United States if I gave up.

That thought alone angered me, angered me so much that I stopped thinking. Sagan's mental attack was still brutal, but I found myself caring less and less about the pain he was inflicting on my mind. All I wanted to do was defeat Sagan, regardless of what price I had to pay to do it.

Gritting my teeth, I started rising to my feet. It was hard and slow, like trying to rise out of quicksand, but I was making some progress nonetheless. The anger flowing through me was giving me the strength I needed to stand.

But then Sagan's shoe came out of nowhere and struck me in the side. The blow knocked me to the pavement, making me gasp in pain.

"Oh, no, you don't," said Sagan, though I caught a hint of worry in his voice. "You must stay down. Stay down and let me turn your mind into mush."

Stay down ... the words echoed through my mind, or what was left of it. It was a soothing, easy command that made me want to close my eyes and take a long nap. And if I didn't wake up, well, that would be okay.

But then my anger rose again. No, I would *not* stay down. I started rising again, this time with more success than before. Inch by inch, I pushed myself up, my anger flowing through my body like hot lava, forcing me to keep going even when my mind told me to stay down.

"What?" said Sagan in shock. "Stupid boy. I said stay *down*."

I noticed Sagan's fist coming at me from the side. Before Sagan's fist hit me, I caught it and, without another thought, twisted it hard.

A loud *crack* followed, and then Sagan screamed in pain. Immediately, the screaming and crashing sounds in my head vanished and my thinking suddenly cleared. My mind felt just as clear as it had seconds ago, making me feel refreshed and happy, but I didn't let go of Sagan's arm.

As I rose to my feet, I forced Sagan down, continuing to twist his arm in the most painful way possible. I didn't even have to use my super strength. Sagan was just so weak that he slowly went down to his knees, tears flowing from his eyes as he screamed in pain.

"Let go, damn it, let go!" Sagan screamed. "You're hurting me!"

"Do I look like I care?" I said. "I caught you, Sagan. You're going to jail. And there's not a thing you can do about it. Soon, everyone in the world will know what you did and your entire cult will go down with you."

Suddenly, Sagan smiled. "Will they, boy?"

I didn't understand what Sagan was talking about, but then I heard the clicking of a gun behind me. Thinking someone was about to shoot me, I activated my super speed and zoomed to the side just as a gun shot rang through the air.

Stopping several feet away from Sagan, I watched as the bullet shot through the air and went through Sagan's skull at an odd angle. Sagan let out one last gasp before he collapsed onto the street, blood leaking out of his head, his arm still twisted at an unnatural angle.

I looked in the direction that the bullet had come from and saw June—her head still bruised from where I'd hit her—standing there, pointing her gun at Sagan. She was staring at Sagan's limp body, her entire form frozen in shock, as if she could not comprehend what she had just done.

"V-Visionary?" said June, her lips trembling. "No … what have I done …"

At that moment, the door to the studio burst open and half a dozen security guards and Secret Service agents ran out of it. But June didn't even look at them. She was just staring at Sagan's still body and at the blood pooling around his head as if it was the only thing in the world.

I stepped back as the Secret Service and security guards swarmed June like locusts. They took her gun away and shackled her with handcuffs. June didn't even try to fight back. She seemed too shocked by what she had done to Sagan to even realize what was going on.

One of the Secret Service agents—a tall, well-built man who was much bigger than me—turned to look at me as the other agents and guards took June away. "Who are you and what happened here?"

"I'm Bolt," I said. I gestured at Sagan. "And Senator Sagan's assistant, June, shot him in an attempt to shoot me."

A couple of agents were surrounding Sagan, with one of them calling for an ambulance on his phone. The agent standing in front of me was frowning, like he wasn't sure whether to trust me or not. "Well, Bolt, you should come with me into the studio. You need to tell me everything that happened out here after June exited the studio with the Senator."

I nodded and followed the agent back to the studio, but not without looking over my shoulder at Sagan's still and unmoving body, feeling grateful that I had not suffered that fate.

THE SUPERHERO'S TEAM

CHAPTER SEVENTEEN

According to the agent—whose name was Tom Silence—no one was killed or seriously wounded in the smoke bomb attack, except for Plutarch, but even he was going to be okay, because the agents had managed to staunch his wound before it bled out too much and were going to transport him to the same hospital that Sagan was going to be taken to. Agent Silence expected Plutarch to recover, however, because June had not shot him in a vital area and he was definitely going to receive the medical attention he needed very soon.

I told Agent Silence everything that had happened after I pursued June out of the building. He expressed doubts about Sagan being the leader of a cult dedicated to brainwashing young heroes, but I insisted that it was true and that he should interrogate June, who would be able to confirm it. Silence told me that he would do that as soon as possible, because June obviously knew a bit more about the situation than I did.

Because that was all Agent Silence needed to know from me, he allowed me to go, especially since I wasn't involved in any other part of the attack. And I didn't hesitate to leave, because I didn't want Silence to remember some law or something that required that he bring in someone like me for further interrogation.

But before I left, I did do a quick search of the building for Triplet, but was unable to find him. That worried me until I heard a small *beep* on my suit-up watch, which displayed a message from Triplet saying, 'LEFT BUILDING. WILL MEET YOU AT YOUR PARENTS' HOUSE SOON WITH MORE INFO.'

Feeling relieved that Triplet was okay, I flew back home through the dark night sky, which took a couple of hours due to how far away Silvers was from Austin. Because it was so dark when I got back to Silvers, I was able to just land in the backyard of our house without being seen by our sleeping neighbors and enter the house through the back door.

There I was greeted by Mom, who was sitting at the kitchen table, apparently waiting for me to return. She quickly called Dad out of the Lab, and once they were both here, I told them everything that happened at the debate. They listened very closely and anxiously and were shocked when I told them who Visionary was.

"Impossible," said Dad, who was sitting at the end of the kitchen table. He took his glasses off his eyes and rubbed his tired eyes. "How can Sagan be Visionary? It doesn't make sense. He's supposed to be pro-neohero."

"I know it's hard to believe, but he told me so himself," I said. "And he backed it up, too, when he tried to turn me into a vegetable with his mental powers."

"So Plutarch really isn't trying to takeover the United States after all?" said Dad, sounding disappointed as he put his glasses back on.

"I guess not," I said. "I know it sounds kind of weird, but it's true."

"Well, I'm just glad you're okay," said Mom. She suddenly looked around. "But wasn't Triplet with you? Where is he?"

"I don't know," I said. "He sent me a message telling me that he was going to be here soon with 'new info,' but I don't know what that means or when, exactly, he'll be here."

"It means I'll be here right now," said a voice behind me.

We looked over at the door to the kitchen, which stood open. Triplet stood in the doorway, looking as tired as if he had run a mile. His right eye was swollen shut, but other than that he seemed okay. He carried a laptop under his arm, a laptop I had never seen him carrying before. I wondered if it was his.

"Mieko?" said Dad as Triplet closed the door and walked over to the table in a tired way. "How did you get here so quickly? We didn't hear your car pull up to the house."

Triplet pulled something out of his coat pocket and tossed it onto the table. It was a small, metal disk, but I didn't know what it was until Dad said, "Hey, that's one of the teleportation disks I gave you during your first visit. Is that what you used to get back here?"

Triplet nodded. "Yes, but that's not important. What is important is this laptop."

Triplet pulled the laptop from under his arms and placed it on the table. Curious, Mom, Dad, and I looked at it closely, but it looked like a pretty ordinary laptop to me.

"What's so special about this laptop?" I said, looking at Triplet in confusion.

"It's Sagan's personal laptop," said Triplet, a little annoyance in his voice. He tapped the laptop's surface. "I stole it after you stopped Sagan. I broke into his changing room and took it because I believed it would have information pertaining to Vision. That's why I left without telling you; I didn't want the Secret Service or security finding me and taking the laptop before I could get a chance to look at it."

"Won't you need to return it to them at some point?" I said. "I mean, once they find out about Sagan's real identity, won't you get in trouble with the law if you don't give them what is probably a very important piece of evidence?"

"I don't trust the government with this information," said Triplet. "Besides, June will probably tell them everything they need to know and more, because without Sagan to protect her, she's a very weak woman. If they do find out that the laptop is missing, then they will probably assume that someone else stole it during the confusion of the attack."

"Why don't you trust the government with this information?" I said.

"Because I've never trusted the government," said Triplet, shaking his head. "And I suspect that Vision may have infiltrated the government, though perhaps not to the same extent as the NHA."

"Why do you think that?" I said.

"Because some of the documents on this laptop indicate as much," said Triplet. "It doesn't name any names—Sagan was smart about that—but there is a paragraph in one of the documents saying that a member of Vision has been successfully installed in the government. I imagine that this member would do everything in his or her power to 'accidentally' destroy this laptop if the government had possession of it."

"Well, what has the laptop told you about Vision so far?" said Dad.

"Not too much yet, but enough for now," said Triplet. He opened the laptop and got it out of its screen saver, displaying a desktop that had hundreds of icons on it. "I had to dig a bit, since most of the files are either labeled misleadingly or are related only to Sagan's campaign, but I eventually found Sagan's personal journal."

"What did it say?" I said.

Triplet pulled out one of the chairs at the kitchen table and sat on it, a tired look on his face. "From what I've read, I learned that Sagan discovered his mental powers in nineteen eighty-six."

"You mean back when the first superhumans were discovered?" said Dad.

"Exactly," said Triplet. "Apparently, though, he didn't tell anyone about his powers. He was terrified that the government might capture him and experiment on him to figure out how his powers worked, which was why he worked hard to keep it a secret from everyone, including his own family aside from his granddaughter Sarah."

"Not exactly an unreasonable fear, given how much bigotry and ignorance against superhumans existed back then," said Dad. "I remember it all too well."

"Yeah," said Triplet, nodding. "Anyway, I learned from the journal that Sagan eventually became convinced that the inequalities between superhumans and normal humans needed to be corrected. While organizations such as the NHA existed to help keep the superhuman community in check, Sagan was certain that the superhumans would eventually attempt to exterminate all normal humans with their immense power."

"Why would he think that?" I said.

"He was mostly looking at villains like Nuclear Winter and Master Chaos," said Triplet. "You know, the crazy guys who weren't above killing innocent people if it furthered their goals and agendas. Sagan believed that the superhuman community needed one, just one, charismatic leader who hated normal humans to rally behind to convince them that it was their destiny to eliminate all non-powered people."

"So what did Sagan do to stop that?" I said.

"I am still reading through most of his journals, but his first attempt to fix the problem was supporting the Vigilante Criminalization Act of 1996," said Triplet.

"The what?" I said.

"It was a law that was killed before you were born," said Dad, causing me to look at him. He was frowning again. "Long story short, the law was supposed to outlaw all superheroics except for government-approved heroes like the G-Men. Then it turned out that the supervillain Judgment was behind it, which is why it was killed before it could be passed."

"Who is Judgment?" I said.

"I'll tell you later," said Dad in a short tone that told me that Dad wasn't looking forward to talking about it. "Mieko, please continue."

"Okay," said Triplet. He put his hand on the laptop's touch pad and tapped it, opening a document that was full of dense paragraphs. "So when that law failed, Sagan finally lost it. He realized that the law could not stop or control superhumans, nor could it even out the inequalities he witnessed. I'm not entirely sure what happened after that, because Sagan's writings became really incoherent at this point, but he eventually decided to weaken the superhuman community from within."

"How did he plan to do that?" I said.

"By founding Vision and naming himself the Visionary," said Triplet. "He used his mind powers to brainwash certain superhumans influential within the community, like Thaumaturge, into joining his cause. But more sinister than that is the ideology he crafted to support his cult."

"What is it?" I said.

"He called it Visionism," said Triplet. He stopped scrolling down the page and said, "According to Sagan, Visionism is an ideology that proclaims complete and absolute equality between superhumans and normal humans. It claims that there are no inherent biological differences between superhumans and normal humans and that any that appear to exist are nothing more than social constructs that we, as a species, must learn to overcome if we are to achieve true equality between superhumans and normal humans."

"That's basically what the Young Neos told me when I first met them," I said. "Are you telling me that Sagan programmed this belief system into them?"

"If not him, then one of the already brainwashed teachers at the Academy," said Triplet grimly. He looked at the rest of us. "And what is even worse is that Sagan appeared to actually believe it himself. He truly believed that he would lead our country to a utopia in which everyone lived in peace and no one ever had to fear that some freak in a mask with more power than sense would attempt to exterminate them."

"That doesn't sound so bad to me," I said.

"In theory, maybe, but in practice, Sagan carried on an incredibly subversive, brutal, and, in my humble opinion, downright *evil* plan to become society's ruler," said Triplet. "You've seen how crazy believers of Visionism are. They will lie, break the law, and do whatever they can to further their cause no matter how immoral it may be. They'll even kill anyone they deem a threat to their utopia, which, according to Sagan's journal, they've done more than once."

I shuddered, remembering how the Young Neos had tried to kill me just a few days ago. "Is that why Sagan was running for President? In order to achieve his goal of a utopia?"

"Pretty much," said Triplet. "He didn't want to originally, because he thought Visionism itself, once embedded in the 'superhuman subconscious,' as he called it, would be sufficient to 'tame' us and destroy whatever threat we posed to the rest of humanity."

"But he was wrong," I said. "Wasn't he?"

"Yes," said Triplet. "Even though he managed to successfully take control of the Academy and the Young Neos, he realized that there were still thousands or tens of thousands of neoheroes and villains all over the world who did not believe in Visionism. He knew that many superhumans never even looked at the Academy, which meant that they would likely oppose Visionism if they ever learned of it. And that, of course, would make it impossible for Sagan to build the utopia he was working toward."

"So he ran for President in order to become a dictator," said

Dad. He sounded depressed, likely because he was a Sagan supporter.

"Precisely," said Triplet. "His plan, when he got into office, was to orchestrate a false superhuman rebellion and then claim emergency powers in order to squash it and 'save' the country. He intended to use the government to seize control of the Neohero Alliance, the Independent Neoheroes for Justice, and a few other smaller superhuman organizations for 'accountability' purposes, killing or imprisoning any members of those organizations who resisted and replacing their leadership with superhumans loyal to Visionism."

"So Plutarch was never an accomplice to his plans or anything like that?" said Dad hopefully.

"Never," said Triplet. "Sagan always saw Plutarch as a threat, so he tried to have Steel Skin kill him and, later on, discredit him with Firespirit. He actually hired Firespirit to attack his rally, hoping that Plutarch's past association with Firespirit would lead everyone to believe that Plutarch had been behind it. Nail Gun, however, was just supposed to be an old-fashioned assassination, though that obviously failed."

"Was it Sagan who bailed them out of Ultimate Max in the first place?" I said.

"Yeah," said Triplet. "He used Plutarch's name to hide his real identity. And not only that, but Sagan and his granddaughter wiped the minds of Steel Skin and Firespirit in order to make sure that they did not reveal who their real employer was."

"How did he wipe Steel Skin's memories?" I said. "Sagan wasn't at the Plutarch rally."

"Ah, but his granddaughter, Sarah Jane Watson, was," said

Triplet. “Incantation wasn't the only Young Neo there that day. Sarah was there with the anti-Plutarch protestors. She used her own mental powers to wipe Steel Skin's memories after he was defeated and then left before anyone noticed her.”

“So Sarah *does* have powers after all?” I said. “I was told she didn't.”

“Yet another lie from a family that seems to be built on them,” said Triplet, shaking his head. “As it turned out, Sarah was born with mental powers similar to Sagan's own, though not quite as strong. That's incredibly rare, seeing as most children of superhumans rarely take after their parents in terms of the powers they inherit. It is even rarer for grandchildren of superhumans to inherit their grandparents' powers, so Sagan got lucky here.”

“Like with me and Dad,” I said, gesturing at Dad. “How my powers are different from his, even though I'm his son.”

“Right,” said Triplet. “Sarah was a huge believer in Visionism, just like Sagan, so she did whatever her grandfather asked her to do, no matter how vile or immoral it was.”

“Did she campaign for him?” I said.

“Sometimes, but her real mission was far more sinister,” said Triplet. “She joined the Young Neos in order to legitimize the view that normal humans could be 'heroes,' too. She was the first ever 'normal' human to join the Young Neos, though we know, of course, that she was never really normal at all.”

“But why did she have to join?” I said. “Why did Sagan want normal humans to join superhuman teams and organizations?”

“Easy,” said Triplet. “Sagan wanted to weaken and cripple the NHA. By filling the organization with normal humans, that would make it much harder for it to fight back against Sagan once he won the election and became a dictator."

"Because an organization of both normal humans and superhumans would be far weaker than an organization exclusively made up of superhumans," said Dad, realization dawning in his voice. "Especially if those normal humans are followers of Visionism, which would make them more loyal to Sagan than to the NHA or any other superhero organization out there."

"Spot on," said Triplet. "It's one of the most cleverly devised plans I've ever had the displeasure of uncovering, and I have uncovered a lot of clever plans concocted by supervillains over the years. But this one puts all the rest to shame, because in some way, it has worked."

"Worked?" I said. "How? Sagan is dead. With June in custody and with Sagan's files in your possession, it won't be long before everyone, normal humans and superhumans alike, know about Vision and its goals."

It sounded reasonable and logical to me, but Triplet and Dad exchanged doubtful looks. Even Mom looked skeptical at my optimism, which annoyed me because I was sure I hadn't said anything wrong and wasn't sure why they were so skeptical about it.

"What?" I said. "What's the problem? Did I say something wrong?"

Triplet rubbed his forehead. "I agree that we should let the world know about Vision and what it's doing. In fact, I plan to release all of this information on the Internet as soon as I can, but you have to look at this from Sagan's point of view."

"Why should I?" I said. "He's dead."

"I say that because Sagan has been working at this for years," said Triplet. "He didn't just start brainwashing kids last month. He has had his disciples steadily propagating Visionism for two decades now. His ideas have already infected a lot of the younger heroes and a fair amount of the older ones. The NHA and the neohero community in general are probably a lot weaker than they otherwise would be thanks to his ideas."

"But if we reveal his plans to the world, then the NHA will at least investigate Thaumaturge to verify the claims, won't they?" I said.

"Probably, seeing as there are still people in the NHA who aren't under Sagan's control," said Triplet. "But that doesn't change the fact that a lot of people still hold to his ideas. It could lead to some unexpected consequences, maybe even a split in the NHA depending on how many people believe in Sagan's ideas."

"Do you really think that that could happen?" I said.

"I do," said Triplet. He closed laptop. "But that doesn't mean we should keep this information to ourselves. If there's one thing I believe in, it's that the truth must be spread no matter what and regardless of the consequences.

"What do you think will happen to the Young Neos?" I said.

"They'll probably be disbanded," said Triplet. "Especially once it comes out that they tried to murder you and were aiding Sagan in his plans for world domination."

I nodded, but despite that, I still felt a little concerned about that idea. "But they won't be punished, will they? Weren't they just controlled by Sarah? Isn't she the one who really brainwashed them?"

"I'm not sure," said Triplet with a sigh. "No doubt Sarah's

powers have influenced their thoughts, but it is equally possible that they are willing converts to Visionism. We won't know until they're arrested and interrogated."

"Did Sagan's documents say why the Young Neos were trying to recruit me?" I said. "They were really insistent about me joining their team, at least until they tried to kill me."

"There's no mention of you in particular in his journal, but I imagine they tried to brainwash you because you're another young neohero who wasn't under their control already," said Triplet. "And a powerful and famous one, at that. If they had managed to get you on their side, they would have become even stronger than they already are."

Again, I nodded. "Did you learn anything else?"

"That's about it so far," said Triplet. "Like I said, Sagan has thousands of pages' worth of documents. It will take me a while to read and analyze them all."

"Can you share them with me?" said Dad. "I'd like to read them as well."

"Sure," said Triplet. "I'll need all the help I can get to read and understand this stuff."

"Are you going back to New York soon?" I said.

"Tomorrow, yes," said Triplet. "I have to report back to my client. He'll be interested in learning that Plutarch apparently isn't the big bad villain we thought he was."

"You can stay with us for the night," said Dad, gesturing at the kitchen. "We have a guestroom that you can sleep in if you want."

But Triplet stood up and shook his head. "Thanks, Ted, but I don't want to impose. I'll find my own place to sleep for the night."

"All right," said Dad. "But if you are ever in Texas, feel free to drop by and say hello. We're always willing to have you over."

"Thanks," said Triplet.

He picked up the laptop and walked past me. In a second, he was out the door, leaving me, Mom, and Dad all alone in the kitchen.

I didn't know what Mom or Dad were thinking, but I knew that I was thinking about what would happen once the truth about Sagan became known to the general population. Whatever would happen, I hoped we'd be prepared for it.

CHAPTER EIGHTEEN

OVER THE NEXT COUPLE of weeks, things more or less returned to normal, much to my surprise. I went back to school, hanging out with Malcolm and Tara, who had apparently put aside their political differences and were talking to each other again. It seemed like the debate on Monday night had convinced Malcolm that Plutarch wasn't so bad, while Tara had shown some concern over the fact that Sagan had been shot by his own assistant. This was even before I told Malcolm about Sagan's true nature, which put him firmly on the pro-Plutarch side, albeit somewhat reluctantly.

I paid careful attention to the news. I learned that Plutarch had survived his assassination attempt, but was determined to keep campaigning all the way to Election Day, even if it meant having to do so from his hospital room bed. Once news came out that Sagan had been behind the attempted assassination, Plutarch's numbers skyrocketed and he actually won the election in the biggest landslide in US history. I knew that because Dad spent that night almost crying at the thought that Plutarch was going to be our next president, while Mom consoled him as best as she could. I didn't mind too much, even knowing Plutarch's campaign promises, mostly because Plutarch seemed like a decent man to me, despite his bravado and arrogance.

As for Sagan, I learned that he actually survived getting shot in the head, but it left him in a vegetative state. As a result, his campaign manager confirmed that he was withdrawing from the race, which forced Sagan's party to hastily find a replacement candidate who ended up losing horribly to Plutarch. I was shocked that Sagan had survived, but according to the reports, Sagan was unlikely to recover, which probably meant that his powers were inactive, too. That meant that Sagan was no longer a threat, but I still worried that he might experience a miraculous recovery at some point, however unlikely that was.

But I didn't worry about June, who was tried and then put in jail for attempted assassination on Plutarch, among other charges. When I last saw her face on the news, she looked almost suicidal, which made me realize just how loyal she had been to Sagan.

But the most important thing to happen in the aftermath of the election was the release of the Sagan's personal documents onto the Internet, courtesy of Triplet, though he used a pseudonym to hide his real identity.

To say that it was a bombshell was the understatement of the year. Although I was basically outside the neohero community, I learned from Triplet that the NHA leaders had read Sagan's journal, which named Thaumaturge and the other Young Neos as being part of Sagan's plan, and tried to arrest them. But apparently, Thaumaturge and the Young Neos fled Hero Island before they could be caught and their current whereabouts were unknown, though Triplet was searching for them and told me he would keep me up to date on his findings.

While I was worried that Thaumaturge and the Young Neos were still out there somewhere, I was glad to hear that the NHA had tried to arrest them. Triplet said that the NHA was not as infected as he thought and that a lot of NHA members were horrified to learn about the extent to which Vision infiltrated the organization.

But not everyone was happy about what happened to Sagan. I saw a lot of comments online from people who were claiming that this was all a conspiracy to make Sagan look bad, that June's confession was either a lie or an outright conspiracy created by the government to make sure Sagan didn't win the election, and that anyone who believed the 'Sagan Pages,' as the journals became known, was a fool and an idiot.

My alter ego's Neo Ranks page got a ton of hate from Sagan supporters, even though I hadn't actually killed Sagan. The only reason people seemed upset at me was because I happened to be there when Sagan was attacked. Granted, June had said I had broken Sagan's arm, but that seemed like a rather minor thing to get upset about.

What really upset the haters, as far as I could tell, was the revelation that Sagan was basically a supervillain who had been playing them like a fiddle. A lot of comments came from people who claimed to be young neoheroes themselves, who said that they were going to hunt down whoever had leaked the Sagan Pages online and would kill me if they ever saw me in real life. That made me glad that no one really knew my secret identity, because if these guys really were neoheroes, they could easily carry out these threats against me and my family.

As for Vision, Triplet told me that there were rumors going around that Thaumaturge had taken on the title of Visionary and that he had made the Young Neos into his new followers. But most NHA members and neoheroes in general condemned Vision publicly, especially the NHA Leadership Council, who said they would purge any Visionists they found in the NHA. Aside from some anonymous Internet trolls, no one actually came out in support of Vision, which made it hard to tell how many Visionists actually existed. I suspected that a lot of them kept quiet because they didn't want to be rejected by the neohero community, which made it impossible to tell just who was a Visionist and who wasn't.

Despite all that, however, I was glad things were over. I was content at this point to just focus on my studies and lay low for a while, at least until the hate from the Sagan supporters and Visionists died down. My parents didn't even have to tell me to do it this time. I was just so worn out from everything that happened that I wanted to focus on something a little less stressful than exposing a crazy superhuman cult that almost succeeded in electing its leader to the presidency.

Still, every now and then, usually on the weekends, I'd put on my costume and fly somewhere. I generally went out into the wilderness or somewhere private, just to train with my powers. My parents actually didn't mind, even though they still didn't exactly approve of my superheroics. Probably because they knew that there was no way to convince me to stop being a neohero, so they were just going to let me do what I wanted.

One day, about a week after Election Day, I was lifting the massive metal block that I had originally used to learn how to use my super strength. By now, it was pretty easy for me to lift, because I was a lot more experienced with using my super strength, but it still provided me a great challenge anyway. I stood in the middle of an empty field with trees standing around me, which kept me hidden from anyone nearby. Not that there were any people nearby, seeing as this place was located in the middle of nowhere, but I liked the extra privacy it gave me anyway.

I was thinking about how I was going to spend Christmas break when I heard something flying in the sky. I looked up to see a robot flying toward me. I was immediately reminded of Master Chaos's old Chaos bots, so I threw the metal block aside to get ready to fly into the air to fight it.

But as the robot drew closer, I realized that it wasn't actually a robot at all. It was actually a man in a powered armor suit, who was flying toward me on his rocket boots.

I stayed where I was, watching as the armored man slowly landed on the ground. He wore armor that looked like futuristic knight armor and even carried a sword at his side. The armor covered his entire body, including his eyes and face, so I had no idea what he looked like underneath, though he didn't seem like a threat.

The armored man looked at me, his green eyes glowing dully in their sockets. "Hello. Are you Bolt?"

The armored man spoke with a metallic, somewhat monotone voice. It made him sound like a robot, although it was probably due to a voice filter in his helmet or something.

"Yes," I said. I looked around, but did not see anyone else around, so I doubted this was a set up for an ambush. "Who are you?"

"I am Mecha Knight," said the armored man. "Perhaps you have heard of me."

"Mecha Knight?" I said in surprise. "You mean one of the leaders of the Neohero Alliance? That Mecha Knight?"

Mecha Knight nodded. "Affirmative. I worked along with your father, Genius, before he retired. A good man. He helped me refine my power suit's weapons and fighting capabilities in ways that would never have occurred to me."

"How did you find me and what are you doing here?" I said. I immediately started patting my body. "Wait, did someone put a tracker on me or something?"

"No," said Mecha Knight. "Your father told me where to find you."

"Oh," I said as I stopped patting myself. "Wait, why did Dad tell you where to find me? I told him that I wanted to be alone right now."

"Because I have an offer to make to you," said Mecha Knight. "Or rather, the Neohero Alliance has an offer to make, an offer we think you will agree to."

"An offer?" I said. "You mean like money?"

"No," said Mecha Knight flatly. "A different kind of offer that has nothing whatsoever to do with money, though we think it will appeal to you nonetheless."

I frowned at the thought that I wouldn't get any money, but because it wasn't every day that one of the leaders of the NHA came to you with an offer, I said, "All right. I'm listening."

"Good," said Mecha Knight. "As you might know, the Young Neos have been disbanded and its members—Incantation, Hopper, Ghost, Technical, and Sarah Jane Watson—have gone into hiding with Thaumaturge, thanks in no small part to your help."

I shrugged. "What can I say? I'm good at busting superhero conspiracies."

Mecha Knight didn't seem to notice what I said, because he continued, saying, "Also, we are currently reevaluating the curriculum being used to teach at the Academy. Already we have discovered lessons that promote a Visionist worldview. It is distressing to find out how thoroughly the Visionists managed to embed themselves in our organization, to say the least."

"Have you discovered any other Visionists in the NHA?" I said.

"So far, Thaumaturge is the only one we know of, but the investigation is still ongoing," said Mecha Knight. "It is sad that Thaumaturge was corrupted. I knew him well. He was a great hero in his own right. I wish I knew how that had happened, but I suppose what matters now is apprehending him and throwing him in prison, where he belongs."

Although Mecha Knight spoke in a monotone, I could still hear some sadness in his voice. I knew that Thaumaturge and Mecha Knight were early members of the NHA, so they had probably been close friends. I couldn't imagine what it would be like to be betrayed by a close friend like that.

"Well, I hope you guys catch him," I said. "If you ever need any help, just call me up anytime."

"We won't need to call you if you accept my offer," said Mecha Knight.

"Why not?" I said. I gasped. "Oh, are you going to offer me a position on the NHA? Like, as an actual, full member?"

"No," said Mecha Knight, shaking his head. "You're too young to be a full member yet. We only accept neoheroes who are eighteen years or older. I have been informed by your father that you are seventeen, which puts you just under the age requirement."

My shoulders slumped. "Damn it. So what's your offer, then?"

"We'd like to offer you a position as the new leader of the Young Neos," said Mecha Knight. "Now that Incantation is gone, the position is open and needs to be filled."

"What?" I said. "Me, the leader of the Young Neos? But I thought that the team was disbanded."

"It is, but only temporarily," said Mecha Knight. "We are currently in the process of putting together a new version of the team, this one free of Visionist influence. We think you would make a great leader, if you choose to accept our offer."

I scratched the back of my head. "Wow. That's a very generous offer, but, uh, why me? Don't you have some other young heroes in the Academy who would be more qualified to lead the team than me?"

"We have many good, talented, and skilled students in the Academy, including my nephew, that is true," said Mecha Knight. "But the fact is that nearly every member of the last Young Neos came from the Academy, and yet all of them turned out to be disciples of Visionary. Seeing as we are trying to eliminate Visionist influence in our organization, we thought it would be best to recruit young neoheroes from outside the Academy, who are far less likely to have been influenced by Visionist dogma than our own students, sadly enough."

"I understand," I said. "But why should I be the leader? I

mean, I'm not doubting my own leadership abilities or whatever, but are you sure there isn't someone better than me out there?"

"We are sure," said Mecha Knight. "You see, Bolt, you have more experience than most heroes your age. You fought Master Chaos and Visionary and came out on top, which is something that most superhumans your age have never done. That kind of experience is invaluable."

"I had help," I said. "I—"

"Even with help, those are still impressive accomplishments for a hero your age just the same," said Mecha Knight. "Therefore, we think that you are the perfect candidate to lead the new Young Neos."

I couldn't argue with that logic, but I had to say, "But my parents don't want me to fight crime. They just want me to be an ordinary teenager until I graduate from high school."

"I spoke with Genius and your mother about this before I came here," said Mecha Knight. "They have agreed to let you lead a new team of Young Neos once it is formed."

"Once it is formed?" I said. "It isn't formed yet?"

"Not yet," said Mecha Knight. "We're in the process of selecting new members from outside the Academy. We have several candidates already, but we aren't going to tell you who they are just yet and won't until the team is formed."

"Okay," I said. "But did my parents really agree to let me lead the team? That doesn't seem like them."

"Your parents weren't very pleased or enthusiastic about it, I think," said Mecha Knight. "But they seem to think you will be a neohero no matter what and it would be fruitless for them to try to stop that. It helps, I think, that Genius will be speaking with you every day."

As skeptical as I was, I realized that Mecha Knight was telling the truth. My parents may not have approved of my superheroics, but I guess they had accepted that I was growing up and would soon be on my own and that they couldn't control me anymore. Maybe they saw it as the next step in my growth as a superhero or maybe Dad thought that the NHA could teach me things that he couldn't. Regardless, I had to admit that I liked this change in attitude, if only because it meant I would get to become the superhero I wanted.

"So, what do you say?" said Mecha Knight. "If you are worrying about education, we will be able to provide you with tutors in every subject imaginable. Will you accept the offer or not?"

I looked down at my hands. A part of me wanted desperately to accept this offer, because I knew that if I turned it down, I'd probably never receive it again. A part of me that sounded an awful lot like Dad, however, was asking me if this was what I really wanted. I thought about Malcolm and my parents, who would still be here in Texas while I was up there in New York, but I told myself I'd come down to visit them as often as I could, so that wouldn't be a big issue.

So I looked up at Mecha Knight again and said, "All right. I accept your offer. When will I start?"

"As soon as we assemble the rest of the team," said Mecha Knight. "By my estimates, that should be sometime just before the New Year, so expect to receive a call from us at that time to come to Hero Island to meet your new teammates."

"You mean I can't just go now?" I said in disappointment.

"The situation on Hero Island … isn't exactly safe for you at the moment," said Mecha Knight vaguely. "It would be best if you stayed here in Texas until we call you."

I understood what he was saying. I had a feeling that a lot of people in the NHA weren't exactly happy about how Triplet and I exposed Vision and its goals to the public. Nor were they happy that Sagan was a vegetable. It seemed like most of the NHA's leaders and members were grateful for what we did, but if there were even just a few Visionists yet to be exposed in the leadership or membership, then I probably had more than a few enemies there who would be happy to see me dead.

"All right," I said. "So you will call me around New Year, right?"

"Yes," said Mecha Knight, nodding. "Until then, I suggest that you keep training and getting better, because you will need to be prepared for the challenges that await you as the leader of the Young Neos."

With that, Mecha Knight activated the rockets in his boot and flew into the sky again. I watched him go until he was out of sight, leaving me all alone again in the clearing.

Then I returned to lifting the metal block, but this time, with a smile on my face. I wondered who my future teammates would be and what kind of threats we'd face as a team. All I knew for sure was that I going to keep training, keep practicing, and keep preparing for the day when Mecha Knight called me to Hero Island to meet my new teammates, whoever they may be.

CHAPTER NINETEEN

CADMUS SMITH—DIRECTOR OF the Department of Superpowered Human and Extraterrestrial Beings and leader of the G-Men—sat in his office at the Department's headquarters in Washington, D.C. He was reading a report from Mr. Apollo, one of his agents, who had recently completed an intelligence operation on a terrorist group in the Middle East led by an infamous supervillain who apparently believed that his powers were a gift from Allah. It was dry and boring, but Cadmus preferred reports that way. He had little patience for agents who tried to add rhetorical flourishes to their reports and Mr. Apollo was one of the few agents who agreed with him on that, which was why he always liked Apollo's reports better than the reports that other agents sent him.

But despite enjoying Apollo's impassively written report, Cadmus found his mind wandering. He was thinking about the entire Vision debacle. The President had chided Cadmus for not knowing about Sagan's true nature sooner, because Cadmus was himself a telepath and had read the minds of each candidate prior to the start of the election season in order to make sure none of them were supervillains in disguise.

That Sagan had somehow managed to trick Cadmus into not even noticing his powers was embarrassing, to say the least. Cadmus had even heard rumors that Plutarch was planning to dismiss him as Director and replace him with someone more 'competent,' but Cadmus knew Plutarch wouldn't. If there was something that Plutarch valued, it was efficiency, and Cadmus was always efficient, Sagan notwithstanding.

Then Cadmus felt another mind enter his office. He looked up at the dark corner of his office just in time to see Shade step out of it. She immediately saluted Cadmus when she saw him.

"Sir," said Shade. "I am back from spying on Bolt."

Cadmus frowned before returning his attention to Apollo's report. "Shade, you know I told you to send your updates to me as written reports on a weekly basis, not verbally in person. Your last report was yesterday."

"I know, sir, but I thought this was far too urgent and sensitive news to put into writing, where it could possibly be intercepted by spies or enemies of the G-Men," said Shade. "I just witnessed a conversation between Bolt and Mecha Knight, one of the leaders of the Neohero Alliance."

Cadmus immediately looked up from the report. "Mecha Knight? Are you sure?"

"Absolutely, sir," said Shade, nodding. "I've seen him before. There was no mistaking that mechanical knight armor for anything else."

"What did they talk about?" said Cadmus, lowering the report.

"From what I heard, the NHA is assembling a new version of the Young Neos and they asked Bolt to be the leader," said Shade.

"Bolt accepted the offer and will be joining the team sometime around the New Year, which is when the team will be assembled and Bolt will be allowed to come to Hero Island."

"Interesting," said Cadmus. "Why would they—ah, I see."

"See, sir?" said Shade.

"It's nothing," said Cadmus. "Is that all, Shade?"

"Yes, sir," said Shade. "That's all I heard."

"I see," said Cadmus. He gestured at the dark corner behind her. "Leave and return to spying on Bolt. Keep me updated on this situation as it develops and leave no detail out of your reports, no matter how insignificant it may seem to you."

"Yes, sir," said Shade, though Cadmus heard puzzled thoughts in her head. She clearly didn't understand why Cadmus found this development significant, but she also knew better than to ask him about it, because it was not information she needed to know.

With that, Shade stepped backwards into the darkness and Cadmus felt her mind leave his office. That was how he knew he was alone.

Steepling his fingers together, Cadmus looked at one of the pictures on his desk. It was an old black-and-white photo, showing a young, smiling boy standing next to a tall man in a nice-looking suit. There was another man in the picture, too, a teenager who wasn't related to either the young body or the grown man, who looked far more rebellious than the boy or the man. In the corner of the framed photo was a scrawl that read *Cadmus, Michael, and Jack, New York City 1933.*

"Jack, Jack, Jack," said Cadmus in a low voice. He chuckled. "For the first time in eighty years, you have finally taken me by surprise. Congratulations."

The photo, of course, did not answer. Cadmus just shook his head and returned to reading the report, but now he was thinking about what Shade had just reported and its implications for the future.

The game, it seemed, had changed … and for the first time in decades, Cadmus was not sure if he was prepared to handle it.

-

Continued in *The Superhero's Summit*, now available wherever books are sold.

I hope you enjoyed my little tale. Please don't forget to give this book a quick review on Amazon. Even just a two-word, "Liked it" or "Hated it" review helps so much. Positive or negative, I am grateful for all feedback from my readers. Please just swing over to the book page and toss up your review, since the star rating you leave on the next page won't be visible online. Amazon simply uses that feedback for their internal recommendation engine.

About the Author

Lucas Flint is the pen name that Timothy L. Cerepaka writes superhero novels under. You can find out more by visiting his website at www.lucasflint.com.

Other books by Lucas Flint

The Superhero's Son:

The Superhero's Test

Available wherever books are sold!

Made in the USA
Middletown, DE
20 November 2017